THE ADVENTURES OF PIERS KING

Duncan Novak

dizzyemupublishing.com

DIZZY EMU PUBLISHING

1714 N McCadden Place, Hollywood, Los Angeles 90028

dizzyemupublishing.com

The Adventures of Piers King
Duncan Novak

First published in the United States
in 2022 by Dizzy Emu Publishing

1 3 5 7 9 10 8 6 4 2

dizzyemupublishing.com

THE ADVENTURES OF
PIERS KING

Duncan Novak

The Adventures of Piers King

SUPER OVER BLACK SCREEN:

"The question, O me! so sad, recurring—What good amid these, O me, O life?

Answer.

That you are here—that life exists and identity,

That the powerful play goes on, and you may contribute a verse."

- Walt Whitman

FADE IN:

EXT. TRAIN - DAY

The year is 1899. A speeding locomotive barrels across a bridge.

Two gunfighters stand atop it. Their hands hover over the holsters on their thighs. One is MONTANA SMITH, (35, African American) the stoic and by-the-books cowboy hero.

The other is the BLACK BANDIT, (20, Hispanic) the most notorious masked criminal this side of the Mississippi. She is resourceful, cunning, and dangerous.

Their PONCHOS blow in the wind.

MONTANA
End of the line, partner.

BLACK BANDIT
Y'know, Montana, the only thing different between me and you is what side of the law we're on.

MONTANA
That's the thing you criminals never understand, Bandit... the law always wins.

Their fingers dance around their SIX-SHOOTERS. The wind howls as the sound of the rhythmic thumping of a train barreling over rusty wooden tracks fills the air.

The tension builds...until.

TIME FREEZES.

PIERS KING, (20) a scrappy young college student, appears, standing on top of the train in his pajamas. He paces down the train cars, thinking out loud.

PIERS
No, no, that's stupid. That won't work.

Like a god playing with their sandbox, Piers moves pieces around with his hands. He telekinetically reverses time and manipulates the world.

PIERS (CONT'D)
What if instead, he said-

Time continues normally. Piers stands in deep focus as the story unfolds in front of him.

MONTANA
That's the thing you criminals never understand, Bandit...

Piers stops time with his hands again, further manipulating his world.

PIERS
(chuckling)
No, No, that won't work...man, this is so boring. Who watches westerns anymore?! Hmm...what if...

Time goes in reverse again.

MONTANA
That's the thing you criminals never understand...

Then-

Piers snaps his fingers.

MONTANA (CONT'D)
WHAT IN TARNATION?!!

A MASSIVE SPACE SHIP appears in the sky. Gunships rain down fire on the train.

Black Bandit lets out a cheesy, maniacal laugh.

BLACK BANDIT
Well, well, well, hero! You forgot about my army of Cyber-Samurai!

Piers stands and mouths the words with excitement as Black Bandit talks.

A dropship flies down to the moving train and moves along with it. A TRIO OF NEON CYBERNETIC SAMURAI drops down onto the car in front of the Black Bandit.

A rope slides down from the ship and Black Bandit grabs it.

BLACK BANDIT (CONT'D)
So long, Montana Smith!

The rope zips her up into the ship, and it flies away. The three Samurai approach a desperate Montana.

He whips out his six-shooter and fires at the leading Samurai. It blocks every shot with its BLAZING ORANGE THERMAL KATANA.

Piers playfully mimics their movements as he swings an invisible blade around with his hands.

MONTANA
Uh oh.

But out of nowhere, a GUITAR SOLO booms in the distance. Montana looks up and sees-

RICKY SIX-FINGERS (25, Japanese American) is a charismatic, wildcard, cyberpunk rocker-boy with a metal arm with six fingers. He shreds the guitar as he stands atop a FIRE BREATHING DRAGON that flies down.

[Reference Song: 'Welcome to the Jungle' by Guns N Roses plays.]

RICKY
Woohoo!!!!!!

MONTANA
Well, well, well. Ricky Six-Fingers.

Ricky strikes a BOOMING POWER CHORD as the dragon shoots fire at the train. It burns the Cyber-Samurai to a crisp. Piers watches and moves pieces of the story around at will.

RICKY
Looks like I came just in time, old man.

MONTANA
No time to talk, boy. We got a spaceship to catch.

Montana climbs on top of the dragon. Piers follows.

RICKY
Only if you promise to yee-haw.

Montana sighs.

MONTANA
(dry)
Yeehaw.

RICKY
Yes!

The dragon lifts while Ricky plays more guitar. As they fly up, they dodge laser fire from the Cyber-Samurai gunships and cruisers. The entire train track EXPLODES behind them.

Ricky destroys ships with power chords, Montana shoots them out of the sky with his pistol, and Piers watches his beautiful creation in amazement. The dragon speeds up on a collision course with the main cruiser.

But everything slowly FADES. Piers' expression slowly turns to complete disinterest. As it does, everything turns to DUST, including the dragon he was riding on.

He falls into the Earth as it's sucked into NOTHINGNESS.

INT. PIERS' APARTMENT - PIERS' BEDROOM - NIGHT

Piers sits at his desk in his disorganized room, typing away on his computer. He blankly looks at the screen. His fingers stop moving.

He sighs, leans back, picks up DRUM STICKS and twirls them.

PIERS
Well, looks like I'm done for the night.

He turns his computer off.

PIERS (CONT'D)
Until next time, Montana and Ricky.

Piers gets up and stretches. CLASSIC ROCK POSTERS cover his walls. A stack of MOVIE DVDs sits on his windowsill. An ELECTRONIC DRUMSET hides in the corner with a pack of drumsticks on the ground.

A pile of MANUSCRIPTS lies on his desk. A CAMERA BAG is on the floor. A small TV sits across from his bed.

Clothes and trash cover the floor. A LONGBOARD leans up against the wall with a helmet lying on it.

Piers undresses and falls into bed, looking up at the ceiling. He takes a deep breath in and falls asleep.

A few moments after he falls asleep, the COLORS around him fade. They all melt away like a coat of wet paint being washed off a wall.

This happens while he's asleep until...

Everything turns BLACK AND WHITE.

After a few more beats of him sleeping in this new black and white world, the sun comes up, and the morning arrives. As it does, his bedroom door whips open.

Piers' two roommates jump onto his bed and hit him with pillows.

ROOMMATES
HAPPY BIRTHDAY!!!

They scream and yell at him, startling Piers.

PIERS
(playfully)
Alright, alright, get off, get off!!

As Piers gets up and out of bed, ALEX MARTINEZ (22) and OLIVER COHEN (21) stand in front of him.

But as one of them starts speaking, something seems off. Suddenly, everything moves in slow motion. Piers looks confused, frustrated, and even scared.

ALEX
Piers! Piers!

Piers snaps out of it.

PIERS
Yeah? What's up?

OLIVER
You're 20! We gotta celebrate! Come on!!!

Piers sits back down on the bed.

PIERS
Or...I could go back to bed.

Alex and Oliver roughhouse with him until they eventually yank the covers off and practically pull him out of bed.

SHERMAN, Piers' French bulldog, comes in and barks, joining in on the fun.

OLIVER
See? Even Sherman wants you to have fun for once.

ALEX
And we all know Sherman is the real man of the house.

OLIVER
(whispering to Alex)
Sherman's a dog.

ALEX
(whispering back)
Shut up.

Piers sighs.

PIERS
Well, if Sherman says so, I GUESS I WILL.

The roommates yell with excitement.

OLIVER
Come on, big man, let's go!

They all hassle Piers as he unenthusiastically gets dressed.

PIERS
Alright, alright, I'm ready.

OLIVER
Woah, woah, woah. I'm not letting you go until you cheer up. No "sad Piers" today.

Piers gives him a fake toothy smile.

ALEX
Oliver, lay off.

OLIVER
Okay, okay. Come on! Let's go!

EXT. BOSTON LOCATIONS - DAY

MONTAGE:

The roommates take Piers on a plethora of adventures around Boston. They go out to eat, walk the Common, go to the beach, visit the zoo, see the city, mess around in grocery stores...juvenile college kid stuff.

Piers is stone cold throughout the entire day. He is apathetic, aloof, and bored. He feels nothing.

INT. PIERS' APARTMENT - ENTRANCE STAIRS - NIGHT

They all arrive at the steps of their apartment building and go inside. As they climb the stairs to their place, Piers stands at the front of the group. Alex and Oliver are right behind him.

ALEX
(quietly)
You okay, bro?

PIERS
Yeah, I'm okay. I'm just tired, that's all.

ALEX
Okay, okay.

Piers slowly opens the door and walks into the dark living space.

INT. PIERS' APARTMENT - LIVING ROOM - NIGHT

Piers turns on the light.

PARTYGOERS
HAPPY BIRTHDAY!!!!

Oliver has set up a final surprise house party for him to celebrate the night. A huge number of people have shown up. Some are friends, but most are acquaintances.

OLIVER
Let's party!!!

The party begins as music blasts and people cheer.

INT. PIERS' APARTMENT - PIERS' BEDROOM - LATER THAT NIGHT

Piers sighs in relief as he closes the door and enters the safety of his bedroom. Sherman, who was lying on the bed, perks up with excitement.

Piers pets Sherman for a bit before sitting at his desk and laying his fingers on the keyboard.

He types lethargically, going letter by letter. He sighs with disappointment.

PIERS
Come on, man. Just...write! Write!! WRITE!!

Nothing.

Fuming with frustration, Piers picks up Sherman and goes to the fire escape.

EXT. PIERS' APARTMENT - ROOF - NIGHT

Piers and Sherman get to the roof of his apartment. He sits in one of two lawn chairs that populate the roof. He looks out at the city skyline. It's beautiful.

After a few moments, Piers hears someone climb to the roof.

It's Alex.

ALEX
Hey, Piers.

PIERS
Hey, Alex.

ALEX
How are you doing?

PIERS
I'm okay. Just needed to get some fresh air.

Alex moves Sherman off the chair and sits down.

PIERS (CONT'D)
He's not gonna forget that. He holds grudges, you know.

Alex gives him a look. Piers sighs.

ALEX
You know we were just trying to cheer you up.

PIERS
I know. It's just...hard when no one can understand.

ALEX
Understand what? You're not alone, you know that? We're trying to help you, dude. We've all gone through things like this. All you do is walk around being sad all day and it's not cool! For once in your life just enjoy yourself! Look at you! You have NOTHING to be sad about. So get up and have fun! You know how much work Oliver and I put in for you to be happy on your birthday?

Alex waits for a response but gets nothing.

ALEX (CONT'D)
Piers, I love you, and I really want to help you. But I don't know how. I just wish you knew how hard this is for me and Ollie.

PIERS
(upset, offended)
You're just saying that! You don't understand what it feels like when all the food you used to love tastes like cardboard...or when the videogames you used to love years ago feel like chores...or when the one thing you always loved doing becomes unbearable...or when the people you love to see every day slowly become...I don't know...fuzzy. They fade out of existence. Everything does. How can I be happy if I can't feel?!!

Alex takes it all in.

ALEX
What about your writing? Don't you enjoy that?

PIERS
I try. But it feels like my imagination is completely...drained. I feel like I have to trick my brain into enjoying anything.

Alex desperately looks for answers.

ALEX
I know what you're gonna say...but I really think you should go to therapy.

Piers throws up his arms.

PIERS
Oh, come on-

ALEX
(getting frustrated)
The school has great counselors included with your tuition!

PIERS
(growing angry)
I'm not going to therapy, Alex!

Silence.

PIERS (CONT'D)
My Dad did. And I had to bury him.

Alex stares at his friend while on the verge of tears.

PIERS (CONT'D)
It's like the rain, Alex. Sometimes, without any warning, it just starts pouring.

ALEX
(softly)
Then what?

PIERS
I just sit on the curb, getting soaked...wishing I had an umbrella.

The boys sit in silence, staring out at the night sky in front of them.

ALEX
Well, Oli's probably wondering where I am right now, so I'm gonna head back downstairs if you wanna come.

PIERS
Yeah, I'll be down in a second.

Alex leaves...but he stops right before heading down the stairs. He turns.

ALEX
You sure you're gonna be okay?

PIERS
I'll be okay. Thanks.

Alex nods and then heads down, leaving Piers alone. He sighs as Sherman sits beside him.

PIERS (CONT'D)
I don't understand, Sherman. Where's my Empire? Where's my Agent Smith? Where's my great adventure?

He looks to Sherman for an answer.

PIERS (CONT'D)
Eh, what do you know?

He picks Sherman up and heads for the stairs.

INT. PIERS' APARTMENT - PIERS' BEDROOM - NIGHT

Piers returns to his bedroom and sits down at his desk. He opens his computer and goes to his script.

PIERS
(sarcastically)
Alright, Piers. Let's make some movie magic.

He types away on his computer until-

EVERYTHING GOES BLACK.

EXT. THE DRIED DESERT - DAY

Piers wakes up on a dried-up desert. He's confused, looking around for any sign of the old world.

Everything around him is still completely BLACK AND WHITE. But Piers is now FULLY COLORED.

PIERS
Uh...what just happened?

All of a sudden, three DROPSHIPS fly down to Piers.

PIERS (CONT'D)
Woah...

They hover in front of him and open their ramps.

Two CYBER-SAMURAI drop from each ship, brandishing glowing neon samurai weapons and armor, the exact same as the ones in his story.

THE BLACK BANDIT herself drops from one of the ships, brandishing ION SIX-SHOOTERS and cybernetic cowboy armor.

BLACK BANDIT
Piers King. You're coming with me.

Piers stands in awe.

PIERS
You're the Black Bandit.

BLACK BANDIT
And you're a wanted man.

PIERS
What? Look, I have no idea what's going on. Please, if you can just help me get a sense of-

BLACK BANDIT
Enough chit-chat, boy. I can bring you in hot...or cold. Your choice.

PIERS
Enough!

Piers gets up and awkwardly attempts to telekinetically move things around with his hands, just as he did in the beginning. Nothing happens.

PIERS (CONT'D)
Uh oh.

Black Bandit COCKS her gun.

BLACK BANDIT
Alright then. Cold it is.

PIERS
Wait, no!

CRACK!

The Black Bandit is SHOT in the back and she falls forward, revealing-

MONTANA SMITH. He rides a beautiful black and white stallion named DOMINO. He carries a LEVER-ACTION RIFLE.

MONTANA
Piers King! I'm here to rescue you!

Piers looks up in wonder.

[Reference Song: 'Immigrant Song' by Led Zeppelin plays.]

PIERS
No shot.

MONTANA
DOMINO! YAH!

Domino barrels past the Cyber-Samurai and toward Piers. The cowboy holds out his arm and Piers grabs it. Piers pulls himself onto the back of the horse as it gallops.

The Black Bandit gets up and shoots at Montana as he rides away, but she misses.

BLACK BANDIT
After them!!

The Black Bandit and the squad of samurai pile into the three ships and boost toward them.

PIERS
(still in awe)
You're Montana Smith!

MONTANA
You got that right, Hoss.

The ships close in and blast laser fire at them, barely missing. Montana evades each blast with subdued style.

They ride toward TOWERING DESERT ROCK FORMATIONS.

The cowboy presses his fingers to his ear, answering comms.

MONTANA (CONT'D)
I've got the boy. Moving to the extraction point.

PIERS
WHAT IS GOING ON?!

Montana takes a six-shooter from his holster, stylishly swings it around his finger, then holds it up.

MONTANA
Here! Take this!

He hands it off to Piers, who fumbles around with it in his hands.

PIERS
I've never shot a gun before!

MONTANA
Time to learn, Hoss!

Piers takes a shot at one of the pursuing ships but MISSES completely. The recoil of the gun causes him to nearly drop it.

MONTANA (CONT'D)
Be careful, now!

PIERS
I'm trying!

Piers takes another shot, MISSING. Laser fire STUMBLES Domino, nearly taking them down.

PIERS (CONT'D)
You got a plan?!

MONTANA
Always!

Montana steers toward one of the rock formations that has a slim opening in it. Domino gallops inside of it.

One of the ships tries to fit into the cave, but it EXPLODES upon impact.

Two pairs of Cyber-Samurai from each remaining ship jump out. They activate their ION BOARDS, skateboard-like machines that can hover in mid-air. They SURF into the rock cave with their weapons equipped.

INT. ROCK CAVE - DAY

Beams of energy emit from the back of the Ion Boards as the Cyber-Samurai surf after Montana and Piers.

They close in on the heroes. Piers fires, again and again, missing each time.

The chase continues through the rough terrain, showcasing Montana's skill on horseback. Piers struggles to hold on.

Through clever fighting, Montana eliminates all samurai but one. Piers checks the chamber of the gun.

ONE SHOT LEFT. He carefully aims the pistol, closes one eye, and-

BANG!

He gets him! Piers cheers.

PIERS
I got him!

A hovering dropship guards the exit to the outside world. It aims its blasters directly at the two heroes.

MONTANA
Good! Now duck!

Piers sees the ship and ducks his head down. It fires a HUGE laser bolt at Montana. The cowboy LEANS BACK, and the laser misses his head by an inch.

By the time he sits back up, his rifle is already cocked. He fires at the ship, and the shot lands. The ship EXPLODES as the two heroes ride out of the cave and into the open.

EXT. THE DRIED DESERT - DAY

They ride through the open desert again. Piers looks behind him as the last ship flies off into the sky.

PIERS
She's pulling back! We lost her!

Montana looks ahead, squinting his eyes.

MONTANA
(quietly)
It ain't ever that simple, Hoss.

Montana and Piers ride off into the sunset.

INT. SHADOW'S CASTLE - MAIN BUILDING - DAY

Guards escort Black Bandit across decorated halls that bustle with Cyber-Samurai soldiers.

INT. SHADOW'S CASTLE - MAIN BUILDING - THRONE ROOM - DAY

Black Bandit walks to the altar of a beautiful throne room. She kneels on the steps.

BLACK BANDIT
Lord Shadow.

SHADOW stands tall in BLACK AND RED CYBERNETIC ARMOR and dons a black cloak. The general of the Cyber-Samurai armies, it is a genderless entity of despair.

It brandishes the STORM-REAPER. The weapon wraps around its shoulders like a python. On an impulse, it can be controlled telepathically and morphed into a sword, spear, or axe.

Shadow speaks with a terrifying, booming voice, switching between tones and pitches that are male and female, creating a cacophonous resonation of sound.

SHADOW
You failed to capture the boy.

Black Bandit nervously shifts.

BLACK BANDIT
Montana Smith rescued him.

The Storm-Reaper slithers around Shadow's body.

SHADOW
You should've stayed on them. Montana could be anywhere with the boy now.

BLACK BANDIT
We'll find him. He'll have to show his face eventually.

The Storm-Reaper slithers off Shadow's body and down toward the floor. It makes its way toward the Black Bandit. She eyes it, terrified.

SHADOW
You don't seem to understand, girl. I want him destroyed before anyone knows of his existence.

The weapon slithers across Black Bandit's legs and up her body.

BLACK BANDIT
Is the prophecy true?

It slithers around her neck and tightens, choking her. She falls to her side and wildly claws at it.

SHADOW
I have commanded the most powerful legions the universe has ever seen. I have conquered the greatest worlds known to man. I have destroyed an infinite number of prophecies.

The Storm-Reaper tightens even more.

SHADOW (CONT'D)
This boy will learn, as did countless messiahs before him...the more he struggles, the more he reasons, the more he loses himself to my grip.

The Storm-Reaper releases from the Bandit's throat. She hacks and coughs.

SHADOW (CONT'D)
I must prepare for the Catalyst. It requires my full attention. Find the boy. Or you will suffer the same fate he will.

Cyber-Samurai guards grab her and drag her out.

EXT. THE CLIFFS - SUNSET

Piers and Montana ride to the edge of a cliff.

MONTANA
Welcome to The Stone Plains.

Piers looks up in wonder as MASSIVE STONE GOLEMS with heads that reach the clouds wander the plains ahead. Sunlight peaks through the cracks and gaps in their stone bodies.

PIERS
No shot.

EXT. THE STONE PLAINS - SUNSET

Piers and Montana ride through The Stone Plains. The grass is dry and yellow. All the plants are dying.

PIERS
This is...drier than I imagined it.

MONTANA
You'll find that most things are different from when you last imagined them.

Piers sees that some of the Stone Golems have DIED. Their bodies are buried under the great plains by their Golem families.

Montana rides onto the outstretched hand of a Golem. It slowly lifts them into the air. It brings them up to eye level, and they stare into its face.

PIERS
They're beautiful.

But then, out of nowhere, a SPACE CRUISER flies through the clouds directly above them. Piers looks up in amazement. He recognizes the ship.

PIERS (CONT'D)
It's the Odessa!

As he says this, Montana rides Domino up the Golem's arm, across its neck and shoulders, and up its other arm as it points upward toward the sky.

The Odessa opens up its ramp for Piers and Montana as they ride up the arm. Domino leaps off the outstretched finger of the Golem and onto the open ramp of the stationary cruiser.

INT. THE ODESSA - BACK HANGAR - SAME TIME

Montana and Piers ride into a hangar full of workers. Despite the large crew on the ship, there is no real work getting done. As soon as they ride in, everyone stops and stares at Piers. He is the only person in FULL COLOR.

Montana hops off Domino and helps Piers off when he sees that he struggles to dismount.

PIERS
Thanks, Montana.

MONTANA
Anytime, Hoss.

Two women approach the heroes. One is CERRA, (47) the battle-worn captain of the Odessa.

The other is ALANA (23). Angelically beautiful and ruthlessly tough, she is the warrior princess of the Space Pirates. She is tall and speaks with a deep Irish accent.

CERRA
Well, well, well. It's the creator himself. Welcome to the Odessa.

PIERS
You're...you're...

CERRA
Cerra, captain of the ship. This lovely lass is Alana, me First Mate.

PIERS
(in awe)
You guys are real.

ALANA
(spiteful)
As real as ye are.

Her comment bites.

CERRA
Montana, meet me on the bridge and get me up to speed. Alana, introduce our new landlubber to the crew of his new home.

ALANA
Aye, aye, captain.

Alana clicks her teeth and jerks her head, signaling Piers to follow her. Cerra and Montana walk off.

INT. THE ODESSA - NIGHT

Alana leads Piers through the ship.

She walks ahead of him. Piers can barely keep up with her.

ALANA
You move like your three sheets to the wind, lad.

Alana doesn't turn when she speaks to him. She's dismissive.

PIERS
Sorry. I'm just...confused.
Shouldn't the crew be working?

ALANA
You left the world in a bad place,
creator.

INT. THE ODESSA - CONCERT VENUE - NIGHT

Alana and Piers enter an empty concert venue.

The only sound is the TUNING of an electric guitar. RICKY SIX-FINGERS lies on the stage in the spotlight. He reads a PIECE OF PAPER.

ALANA
Ahoy!

RICKY
Alana, honey, you know what we said
about pirate talk when you're in
the venue! If I catch you saying
any of that sea-shanty-davy-jones-
locker crap I swear I'll-

Alana clears her throat. Ricky sits up, his LONG BLACK HAIR disheveled and dangling over his piercing eyes. As soon as he sees Piers, his eyes go wide.

RICKY (CONT'D)
(slyly)
Well, well, well. Daddy's home.

Piers shifts awkwardly.

PIERS
(to Alana, whispering)
Is he talking about me?

RICKY
You gave me super hearing,
remember? And yes, I am talking
about you, you little shrimp.

ALANA
Captain wants us on the bridge now,
savvy?

RICKY
Oh, I "savvy," sweetheart. Tell Cerra I'm busy practicing.

ALANA
This is important.

RICKY
So is this.

PIERS
Your guitar isn't even tuned yet.

Ricky gets up and jumps off the stage. He slowly approaches Piers.

RICKY
Well, maybe I was just starting. And even though you think you can order us around and do whatever you want to us in whatever world you came from...here, the rules are different. So you better buckle up shrimp-boy. You're in our fish tank now.

Ricky stands close to Alana and Piers. Now realizing he's up and off the stage, he pushes past them and leaves the venue.

ALANA
See you on the bridge!

Piers looks at Alana.

PIERS
Shrimp boy? Was that supposed to be clever?

ALANA
Get used to it.

Frustrated, Piers runs out of the venue. This catches Alana off guard. She chases after him.

INT. THE ODESSA - BRIDGE - NIGHT

Piers stomps through the doors and into the bridge. Alana runs up behind him.

Cerra, Montana, and Ricky stand near the HOLOGRAPHIC MAP PROJECTOR in the middle of the room.

PIERS
Alright, I've had enough!! I'm sick and tired of asking questions and not getting any answers! What is going on?!

They all look at him.

PIERS (CONT'D)
Look, I get it now! For whatever reason, you all don't like me. But obviously, you need me for something! So, just tell me what I need to do so I can get out of here and go back to my normal, crappy life!

Cerra steps forward.

CERRA
Years ago, our world, the one ye created, was full of color, teeming with life. That was until the Shadow arrived with its bilge-sucking army of Cyber-Samurai.

A projection of SHADOW appears. It's TERRIFYING, sending chills down Piers' spine.

CERRA (CONT'D)
Ever since it arrived, it's been conquering the realm, washing the color out of everything. It rules through fear and terror, bringing apathy to all those it rules over.

PIERS
But I don't understand. I created you all. I never wrote someone named "The Shadow." Where did it come from?

CERRA
Every story needs a villain, lad. This is ours.

PIERS
But how are you acting autonomously? Don't characters have arcs? How is this going on without me? Why can't I just...control you all?

RICKY
Kid, you may have written our outlines on your world, but down here, we're just as real as you wish you could've written us. So get used to it, "creator."

PIERS
(regretful)
I never finished your stories.

RICKY
Yeah, thanks a lot. Now, look at our world.

CERRA
You're the creator, lad, the only one left with color. If ye want to gain the power over us that ye once had, ye have to finish our stories and restore balance, freeing our world from the Shadow.

PIERS
And what if I fail? You'll all be destroyed?

CERRA
In one month, The Shadow will complete what it calls, "The Catalyst." If the Catalyst happens, its shadow energy will completely engulf our entire world, dooming every one of its inhabitants to lead a life without purpose, hope, or energy...it will leave our world in darkness and apathy for all of existence.

Piers crouches down. He puts his head in his hands.

PIERS
This is not a crossover I expected.

Montana looks at the boy, concerned.

MONTANA
Are you alright, son?

PIERS
No, I'm pretty far from alright! What? You expect me to defeat some all-powerful supervillain who's literally conquered the world?!
(MORE)

PIERS (CONT'D)
I'm just a kid! I'm supposed to be your god, but I don't have any powers! I can barely even get out of bed in the morning and now, all of a sudden, I'm supposed to be a hero?

Silence. The crew all exchange nervous glances.

PIERS (CONT'D)
None of you believe in me, do you?

CERRA
Truthfully, lad...we've run out of any other options. We're desperate.

PIERS
I appreciate the vote of confidence, Captain.

RICKY
(sardonic)
Anything for our messiah!

MONTANA
Hush up, Ricky!

Montana walks up to a panicking Piers and calms him down.

MONTANA (CONT'D)
(whispering)
We live in a broken world, Hoss. Now I don't know about them boys and girls but I'm with you all the way, come hell or high water. You're all we got. Please.

Piers looks up at Montana and nods. He stands and looks around the room.

PIERS
Okay. Let's finish your stories.

[Reference Song: 'You've Got Another Thing Coming' by Judas Priest plays.]

Piers goes toward the holographic display.

PIERS (CONT'D)
This thing got a map or something?

Cerra projects a map of the ENTIRE WORLD. It shows which regions are under the Shadow's Reign.

EVERYTHING IS.

PIERS (CONT'D)
If we're gonna write this story, we're gonna need an outline.

Piers recognizes THREE of the major stronghold/geographic sectors of the world.

PIERS (CONT'D)
(thinking out loud)
Okay, this is good. It seems this world has been divided into three sectors, all based on locations I've written in screenplays and stories before.

RICKY
Unfinished stories.

Piers gives Ricky a look.

PIERS
Each one of you comes from one of these locations which means...

ALANA
All hands on deck.

PIERS
Exactly. We'll work our way from top to bottom, from the cloud civilization of Mrak to the Forests of Keda. And after we've liberated the three sectors, we'll rally the people and lay siege to Shadow's castle and go home safe and sound.

He scans the room.

PIERS (CONT'D)
(timidly)
How was that? Did...did I do alright?

CERRA
How exactly are ye going to liberate each district?

PIERS
(cheeky)
We'll just do whatever feels natural.

MONTANA
What?

PIERS
Sorry. It's a...filmmaking thing...we'll figure it out.

MONTANA
What about The Bandit and her army? They'll be huntin' us. The Odessa ain't exactly hard to find.

CERRA
We'll drop you off in Mrak and you'll have to travel yourselves.

Ricky looks at her with concern.

CERRA (CONT'D)
Something to add, Ricky?

RICKY
No, ma'am.

CERRA
It's settled then. We'll set course for Mrak. In the meantime, get some rest. You'll need it.

They all exit the room. Ricky gives Cerra a confused look on the way out.

INT. THE ODESSA - CONTINUOUS

As they walk out of the bridge, Ricky catches up with Piers and YANKS him aside.

RICKY
I don't care who you are or if you birthed me into this so-called existence or not...if my home is destroyed because of you, I'll make sure you regret it, shrimp.

ALANA
Ricky, enough!

Ricky lets go of Piers' arm and storms off.

ALANA (CONT'D)
What did he say to you?

PIERS
I don't know...something about his guitar.

ALANA
Yeah, that sounds like him.

Piers watches Ricky carefully.

INT. THE ODESSA - QUARTERS - NIGHT

Alana leads an exhausted Piers into a small bedroom.

ALANA
Here's where you can bunk until we reach Mrak.

PIERS
Thanks.

Piers gets settled in. He chuckles.

PIERS (CONT'D)
You know, I never wrote you to be a pirate.

ALANA
Sorry to disappoint.

Alana heads for the door.

PIERS
Is something wrong?

Alana turns. She sighs.

ALANA
When I thought of whoever or whatever was responsible for the creation of me life and the universe around me, I thought of an omnipotent, all-powerful being. Turns out it's just a child.

PIERS
I'm sorry. I just don't wanna be a burden.

ALANA
I just...really hope you know what you're doing.

Alana closes the door, leaving Piers alone. He slouches and lies back on the bed.

PIERS
I have no idea what I'm doing.

DARK SHADOWS creep into the room. Piers feels an unnerving and overwhelming sense of TERROR.

He SCREAMS. WHISPERS and HIGH-PITCH SCREECHES ring through his ears. Black smoke fills the room. Then-

THE SHADOW APPEARS.

SHADOW
You can't escape me, Piers. I will follow you everywhere you go.

PIERS
NO! NO! GET AWAY! HELP!! HELP!!

Then, nothing. Piers lies on the floor in the fetal position, crying.

INT. THE ODESSA - CONCERT VENUE - DAY

Piers aims down the sight of a six-shooter while Montana watches him closely.

MONTANA
Steady now...don't anticipate it...steady...strong stance...

Piers throws his hands up and looks at Montana.

MONTANA (CONT'D)
Go on!

Piers looks down the gun and fires. HIT!

MONTANA (CONT'D)
Good shootin' Hoss.

PIERS
Yeah. It only took 3,000 tries.

MONTANA
We all start somewhere.

Ricky enters the room.

RICKY
Hey, cowboys! Paradise awaits!

They look at each other and run after Ricky.

EXT. THE ODESSA - RAMP - DAY

The ramp opens, revealing the four heroes. Alana stands proud in her PIRATE UNIFORM. Montana wears his COWBOY PONCHO with Domino by his side. Ricky wears his ROCKER-BOY CLOTHES. Piers wears a RUSH T-SHIRT and JEANS.

Cerra walks up to them.

CERRA
We had to drop ye off just outside the gates of Mrak, so you'll have to make the rest of it by foot. I'll see ye all when the world is in color again.

RICKY
(quietly, so no one else can hear)
Promise me you'll stay safe, Cerr.

CERRA
(smirking)
I promise, Ricky.

They both smile and nod at each other. Then, the heroes embark.

EXT. CLOUDS OUTSIDE OF MRAK - DAY

The heroes walk across a sunny cloudscape. Montana rides Domino. Alana walks gracefully across. The other two...not so much.

RICKY
How do you even walk across this crap?

ALANA
Get used to it, Rocker-boy.

RICKY
Yeah, yeah. Whatever.

Eventually, they make it to the huge golden gates of the cloud paradise city-

MRAK.

It's Gondor if it was golden and on a base of clouds. Golden walls shield the city.

EXT. GATES OF MRAK - DAY

A legion of guards in white armor stands at stations above the gate as the heroes approach. The GATE CAPTAIN, a woman of staggering height and strength, stops them.

GATE CAPTAIN
Lo! Who approaches the gate?

ALANA
Don't recognize me?

The Captain stops for a minute. She lets down her guard.

GATE CAPTAIN
We don't recognize banished daughters.

Alana shifts uncomfortably.

ALANA
This is bigger than I am. I seek counsel with the Sovereign.

The Captain notices Piers, the only person with color.

GATE CAPTAIN
The boy. Who is he?

PIERS
My name is Piers King. I am the creator. I've come to rid the land of the Shadow and bring color back to your world. You're the Guardians of the Gate, Mrak's bravest and most cunning warriors. You know power when you see it. That's how I wrote you.

They stop for a second and consider. The Gate Captain signals for them to be let in.

EXT. MRAK - DAY

Mrakian warriors in glistening white armor escort the heroes through the cloud kingdom. Alana PUNCHES Piers in the arm.

ALANA
You could've just let me handle
that, lad.

PIERS
Well, you didn't tell me you were
banished!

RICKY
(butting in)
Yeah, you were TOTALLY handling it.
I mean, I knew you could be high
maintenance and all...but banished?
Phew!

Montana slaps Ricky in the back of the head.

MONTANA
Hush, Ricky.

RICKY
Hey! Hands off the merchandise,
cowboy.

ALANA
I can handle myself, Montana. I
don't need you to white-knight me!

PIERS
Guys! Shut up!

They close in on the beautiful Mrakian Royal Palace.

To Piers' surprise, there is no presence of Cyber-Samurai anywhere.

INT. MRAKIAN ROYAL PALACE - THRONE ROOM - DAY

The heroes reach the Throne Room. It's decked with jewels, beautiful white scenery, and guarded by HUGE ARMORED WOMEN

The famed Sovereign, CELESTE, (50) sits on her cloudy throne. She is cold and calculated.

She doesn't speak in questions...only statements. Her back is turned to them.

CELESTE
So, the banished has returned.

Alana steps forward.

ALANA
Sovereign Celeste.

CELESTE
Do not speak my name. Only true Mrakians hold that privilege. You're nothing but a dirty pirate, a fallen daughter of the greatest civilization this world knows. But I'm sure you don't need a reminder.

She turns around to face them.

CELESTE (CONT'D)
But I see you've brought guests.

Piers steps up to Alana and kneels before Celeste...much to Alana's subtle disgust.

PIERS
Lady in White. It's an honor to be in your presence.

CELESTE
Skip the pleasantries, boy. I know who you are.

PIERS
Then you know why I'm here.

CELESTE
I do. And I'm afraid your attempts will be in vain.

PIERS
And why is that?

CELESTE
The Shadow and its armies agreed to stay out of Mrak as long as we didn't interfere with their conquest. When the color faded, we saw it as a necessary evil for peace, a deterrent that would keep our home safe.

ALANA
While others suffer?!

CELESTE
Silence!

Alana drops her head with reluctant respect.

CELESTE (CONT'D)
We do not concern ourselves with the dealings of the lower worlds.

PIERS
(to himself)
I knew this would happen.
(to Celeste)
This is exactly what the Shadow wants! To trick you into apathy!

CELESTE
A necessary price for peace.

Piers gets desperate.

PIERS
I'm the creator. I made you. That must count for something. You need to believe in me.

CELESTE
I will not thank you for an existence such as this.

Piers doesn't know what to do. Celeste waits for an answer.

ALANA
He will compete in the trials!

PIERS
Trials?

CELESTE
He needs a partner to compete with.

ALANA
I will. If we win, you have to agree to aid us when the time comes.

Celeste thinks about this for a while.

CELESTE
It shall be done. You will compete in the Trials of Mrak tomorrow at sunrise. If the creator is all he says to be, then we shall aid him in his efforts of reunification. Go now.

Celeste turns around as Mrakian guards escort the heroes out.

PIERS
Trials? I don't remember writing anything about trials.

ALANA
Just follow my lead.

EXT. THE MRAKIAN COLOSSEUM - STANDS - SUNRISE

The sun rises over the horizon of the bustling Mrakian Colosseum. Scores of Mrakians sit in the seats and cheer.

Ricky and Montana go through the stands. Mrakian women stare at them as they go by. Most have never seen a man before.

RICKY
You know, cowboy, I could get used to this. You think any of these Mrakian babes have been with a man before?

MONTANA
I doubt what you have to offer is very stimulatin.'

RICKY
Yeah, what do you know?

INT. THE MRAKIAN COLOSSEUM - ARMOR & WEAPONS ROOM - SAME TIME

Alana and Piers gear up for the trials. Alana stares at herself in a mirror on the wall. She looks distressed. Piers is clueless.

PIERS
You think I should go with the Mrakian sword...or spear? You should also probably know that I have literally no fight training at all.

He looks back and notices that Alana is on the verge of panicking.

PIERS (CONT'D)
Alana? Are you okay?

ALANA
No! I'm not okay! I shouldn't have done this. I can't do this.

Tears well in her eyes.

PIERS
Look, I know what it's like to...bottle up everything you're feeling inside. I'm not gonna force you to do anything, but...I think it would really help if you gave me a chance.

Alana nervously runs her hands through her hair.

ALANA
Celeste is my mother. I had a twin sister named Lydia. Being born into royalty in a society of warrior women, people have certain expectations of those in positions of power...expectations that I couldn't meet.

PIERS
I know how you feel.

ALANA
Lydia was the clear choice for the heir to the throne. She was smarter, faster, stronger, taller, more beautiful...she was everything Celeste wanted in a daughter and everything I wanted to be...everything I couldn't be. These trials are a rite of passage for heirs to the throne. Two go in, only one is meant to come out. Everyone expected Lydia to be Sovereign. Everyone wanted her to be Sovereign. I was set up to fail, Piers. Do you know what it's like for your own mother to accept that her daughter is going to die like it's nothing?

Piers listens to every word.

ALANA (CONT'D)
When we took the trials, Lydia was hurt and in trouble. She looked me in the eyes and begged me to help. She begged me for anything. But I just stood there, frozen. My sister died in that arena because of me. Because I was scared...because I was weak. After she died, I refused to continue.
(MORE)

ALANA (CONT'D)
When it was all over, I wasn't even allowed in my own home without being an outsider. So I left. It's my fault that Lydia died that day. It's my fault that Mrak has no heir to the throne. I'm a failure, Piers.

Piers lets this sink in. He pulls her in close.

PIERS
I know what it's like to feel like a failure. But the greatest heroes in stories on my world aren't the ones who succeed the most, but the ones who fail, and get up nonetheless. You're one of them.

Alana looks into his eyes.

PIERS (CONT'D)
When we both come out of this alive, your story will be one of the greatest legends ever told in Mrak. One better than anything I could've ever written.

She smiles.

PIERS (CONT'D)
One that you'll write yourself.

Silence. She puts her hand on his shoulder.

ALANA
Then what are we waiting for, lad? Let's go save the world.

EXT. THE MRAKIAN COLOSSEUM - ARENA - DAY

Alana and Piers walk into the arena. It's set up like an obstacle course. Huge blocks of scattered marble act as vantage points and cover.

They connect to each other like a jungle gym, reaching far up into the sky. Piers looks up in wonder, gawking at the verticality.

On the other side of the colosseum at the top of the stands, Celeste watches, her eyes cold and narrow.

Piers awkwardly shuffles around with a spear in one hand and a sword in the other. Alana carries her personal CUTLASS.

PIERS
You never told me which one to grab, so I just grabbed both.

ALANA
Just stick by me. Whatever happens, we can't lose sight of each other.

PIERS
(cheeky)
Aye, aye.

Alana climbs onto a vantage point. Piers climbs onto another beside her.

ALANA
When it comes, we need to get to the top and grab that helmet.

At the top of the obstacle course, there is a glistening ROMAN STYLE HELMET

PIERS
It?

THE GROUND RUMBLES!

A HUGE WHITE DRAGON BREAKS THROUGH THE GROUND. This is DEGERA. She roars and shoots ICE SPIKES at the heroes.

[Reference Song: 'Saturday Night's Alright (For Fighting)' by Elton John plays.]

PIERS (CONT'D)
AN ICE DRAGON?!! THIS WAS NOT IN MY SCRIPT!

ALANA
Then it's time to improvise!

Piers throws his spear at Degera, but she simply knocks it out of the way with one of her arms. She then SLAMS her tail down on them. The two heroes leap out of the way, barely dodging it.

They both bolt from cover to cover as they try to dodge her ice blasts.

Alana climbs, but as she gets higher, Degera shoots another wave of ice. Her breath creates a HUGE ICE WALL, blocking Alana's path. Five ICE SOLDIERS break out from the wall and engage Alana in combat.

Seeing this, Piers clumsily climbs higher, getting the attention of Degera while Ice Soldiers battle Alana.

EXT. THE MRAKIAN COLOSSEUM - STANDS - SAME TIME

Ricky and Montana watch the battle from the stands. Ricky is captivated by the violence. Montana is concerned.

MONTANA
They need help. They ain't gon' make it.

RICKY
What? Chill out, Tex. They'll be fine.

As he says this, Ice Soldiers overwhelm Alana. Degera SWATS Piers and he falls down multiple marble platforms, nearly falling to his death.

MONTANA
Come on!

Montana moves.

RICKY
Wait! Only if I get to use your lasso.

Montana throws Ricky the lasso and they move down the stands.

EXT. THE MRAKIAN COLOSSEUM - ARENA - SAME TIME

Piers leaps across a gap to another marble platform, nearly falling again. But before he can climb higher, Degera GRABS him and pulls him close. She charges up a huge ice blast.

PIERS
Alana!! Help!!

ALANA
Piers!!

But before Degera roars, she's HIT by a BULLET from below!!

MONTANA
Yee haw!

Degera roars in pain and drops Piers. He screams in fear as he falls, but then-

RICKY CATCHES HIM! Using Montana's lasso, he swings down and catches Piers. They crash down onto the ground below.

The crowd ROARS with applause. Ricky and Piers struggle to get up.

RICKY
(groaning)
You owe me one, shrimp.

Using clever swordplay and her environment to her advantage, Alana destroys the remaining Ice Soldiers.

She sheathes her sword and CLIMBS the marble platforms as the three others engage Degera as a distraction.

Alana eventually climbs to the top, the helmet just a few more jumps away. But then, she looks down.

Montana is swatted away by Degera and is KNOCKED OUT. Ricky is BEATEN by another group of Ice Soldiers. Piers is backed into a corner, his only cover being slowly CHIPPED AWAY by the dragon's ice breath.

Letting out a Mrakian war cry, Alana brandishes her sword, LEAPS off the platform, and dives down through the air until-

SHE SLAMS HER SWORD DOWN INTO DEGERA'S NECK, BRINGING THE DRAGON THROUGH THE GROUND WITH HER.

Moments of silence follow as the heroes emerge from their spots. When the dust settles, they all gather around the giant crater in the ground and look down.

PIERS
No...

They all look down in solemn silence, as Alana climbs out of the crater unseen from a different angle.

ALANA
Ahoy!

They all look over at Alana in utter relief. She limps over to the other heroes as Ricky and Piers cheer and swarm her. Montana gives her a silent nod.

The crowd roars with applause like never before.

PIERS
(hugging Alana)
I knew you could do it.

ALANA
Not without you.

Celeste and her escorts appear from the lower gates and approach the heroes.

ALANA (CONT'D)
Sovereign.

CELESTE
No heir has ever slain Degera before in the history of Mrak. No heir has also ever shown such disrespect for our traditions and rituals.

ALANA
Mother, I-

CELESTE
Silence!
(beat)
I've always believed that being Sovereign was about being the strongest of Mrak. But today, you showed me what it means to have real strength.

She kneels before Alana.

CELESTE (CONT'D)
It would be an honor to call you Sovereign, my daughter.

The crowd kneels before her in the stands.

ALANA
Mother, I wish I could accept. But my destiny is with the creator now.

Celeste stands back up.

CELESTE
Then I shall be waiting for you when you return. Go with him. He will need you. We all will.

They both look at Piers, who stands toward the center of the arena, away from the group. He scans the area. He closes his eyes, kneels down, and touches the ground with his hand. All of a sudden, the ground beneath him shows its COLOR.

Our heroes look around as the entire Mrakian civilization is COLORIZED, revealing its beautiful WHITE AND GOLD TONES.

All Mrakians gain their color, all except Alana. When Piers is finished, he stands and wobbles around.

Alana runs to him and he faints in her arms. Tears stream down her cheeks as she holds him.

All heroes remain in BLACK AND WHITE.

RICKY
Hey, Montana?

MONTANA
Hmm?

RICKY
You think we got any room for a couple of Mrakian girls in our party? I'm starting to think I need a warrior princess in my life if you know what I-

Montana hits Ricky over. He groans in pain.

EXT. GATES OF MRAK - DAY

The Guardians of the Gate kneel before the heroes as they leave Mrak.

ALANA
Wait.
(beat)
Before we go, I wanna show ye all something.

EXT. MRAK - THE LOOKOUT - DAY

Alana leads the heroes out of the palace and to a lookout in the clouds.

She moves forward onto the highest cloud and stares out onto a gorgeous cloudscape.

A few moments pass. Tears stream down her sunlit cheeks. She looks to her side. Piers sulks on the edge of a cloud, looking out into the sky.

ALANA
Beautiful, isn't it?

PIERS
Yeah, I guess.

ALANA
How are you feeling?

PIERS
I'm okay.

ALANA
We just saved Mrak! You're just...okay?

PIERS
It was all you, Alana. I'm just...here.

Piers gives Alana a half-smile, his lips trembling. Alana extends her hand out, and he takes it. They both look into the sun together.

EXT. GATES OF MRAK - DAY

The heroes exit Mrak for the final time. Alana and Celeste nod to each other as they leave.

EXT. THE DRIED DESERT - NIGHT

A detachment of THREE DROPSHIPS flies across The Dried Desert.

INT. BLACK BANDIT'S SHIP - NIGHT

Black Bandit stands on the bridge of her small dropship. She presses a button on a holoprojector. A life-size HOLOGRAM of Shadow appears in the room.

BLACK BANDIT
Lord Shadow. They're moving faster than I anticipated. Piers has already restored color to Mrak. I'm going to order my ships to pursue the Odessa.

LORD SHADOW
No. The boy is moving on foot. I can sense it.

BLACK BANDIT
What are my orders?

LORD SHADOW
They're moving toward Neo-Tokyo. Meet them there. Do not fail me again.

The hologram dissipates, leaving the Black Bandit alone for a few moments.

EXT. THE MOUNTAINS - DAY/NIGHT

MONTAGE:

The heroes journey across snowy mountain peaks. They begin from the cloudy steps of Mrak to the mountain peak entrances and move down the treacherous but captivating landscapes that populate the world.

On their journey, they encounter strange wildlife, cross raging rapids on fallen trees, climb down rocky caverns, etc.

EXT. MOUNTAIN CAMPSITE - SUNSET

The heroes finish setting up a cliffside camp for the night. Alana and Piers practice sword fighting on the cliffside. Montana cleans his lever-action rifle. Cerra's hologram sits across from Ricky.

RICKY
Are you sure everything's okay?

CERRA
Aye, Ricky. I'm sure. Focus on your mission, and I'll focus on mine.

RICKY
I am focusing!

CERRA
Doesn't sound like it, lad.

RICKY
Hey now, call me lad one more time and I might yack.

CERRA
Oh, is the famous rocker-boy too good for affection now? Don't forget where you came from, boyo.

RICKY
Don't worry! I got a great memory.

CERRA
Then maybe ye remember how much of a little crybaby ye were when I first found ye.

RICKY
Okay, I think I got my daily amount of pirate talk in for today. I'll talk to you tomorrow?

CERRA
Same time as always, lad. Good luck.

RICKY
What did I say about-

Laughing, she hangs up. Ricky groans in protest. He picks up the hologram and pops a squat next to Montana.

RICKY (CONT'D)
So...Tex, whaddya think it feels like?

MONTANA
What?

RICKY
To have color again.

MONTANA
Wish I could remember.

RICKY
What's your tragic backstory anyway? What are you hiding?

MONTANA
I ain't talking 'bout it.

Montana moves away to pack his gun into the tent. Ricky follows.

RICKY
Oh come on, can't you tell me anything? What's your home like? Where'd you get your scars? Who's the Black Bandit?

MONTANA
(suddenly, furiously)
I said I ain't talking!!!

Piers and Alana look back, concerned. Ricky, stunned, backs off.

RICKY
Alright, alright. Jeez.

PIERS
Hey, what's your problem, Ricky?

RICKY
Shut up, kid. I don't need lip from you.

Piers gets angry, but Alana pulls him back.

RICKY (CONT'D)
What are you gonna do? Write me out of existence? Gimme a break.

Ricky storms off.

PIERS
I need some rest.

Once Ricky is alone, he sits by a tree and pulls out the same PIECE OF PAPER from the venue. He reads through it.

INT. PIERS' APARTMENT - PIERS' BEDROOM - DAY/NIGHT

Suddenly, Piers wakes up in his apartment, strapped to a chair, staring out his window. Confused and scared, he tries to break free, screaming for help.

Shadow appears behind him and puts its hands on his temples. The window opens and wind blows into the room. Piers stares blankly out the window as days and nights pass by at lightning speed.

EXT. MOUNTAIN CAMPSITE - NIGHT

Piers wakes up in a cold sweat. He examines his surroundings, making absolutely sure that he is back to reality. He sighs and falls back. Tears stream down his cheeks.

EXT. THE MOUNTAINS - DAY

Our heroes walk across another mountain landscape. They stop when they see it.

The huge skyscrapers of NEO-TOKYO stand in the distance. Roads in the sky extend out from the metropolis.

FLYING CARS zoom through the air. Cyber-Samurai patrols hover in the outskirts.

PIERS
No shot.

RICKY
(spiteful)
Home sweet home.
(turning to Piers and Alana)
You two kids are gonna need these. Don't want any Cyber-Samurai patrols spotting you.

He gives two CLOAKS AND MASKS to them. There's a white one for Alana and a black one for Piers.

PIERS
(putting it on)
Where'd you get these?

RICKY
Do you ever stop asking questions?

PIERS
Whatever. Let's go.

The heroes continue forward.

EXT. NEO-TOKYO - BAZAAR - NIGHT

The party of heroes walks through the elevated city streets of Neo-Tokyo, Ricky's cyberpunk metropolis home. The city is oddly sparsely populated. All the shops around them are CLOSED.

ALANA
Where is everyone? Why is everything closed?

RICKY
I don't know. Ask your boyfriend back there.

ALANA
Excuse me?

PIERS
(somewhat excited)
Boyfriend?

RICKY
Did I stutter, princess?

ALANA
You're full of it, Ricky. You know that?

RICKY
Well aware.

ALANA
What are we doing here, anyway? This place is gross!

RICKY
We're visiting an old friend.

The party stops at a BAR. Its neon signs flicker.

ALANA
A bar? Really?

RICKY
I'm sorry, does my home not reach your high standards, your highness? I thought you were a pirate. Or has your sudden change in status killed your pirate accent too?

Alana looks like she's about to explode.

ALANA
No, it's perfect. Let's go.

RICKY
After you.

Alana pushes through Ricky. Montana follows next after dismounting Domino. Piers stands there.

RICKY (CONT'D)
Well?

PIERS
I'm not 21.

Ricky sighs and grabs Piers by the back of the neck and shoves him into the bar.

INT. VARNISH'S BAR - NIGHT

The party of heroes enters the bar. As soon as the patrons see Ricky, they all stare at him with disgust.

RICKY
(whispering)
Just act natural.

Piers immediately heads to a jukebox and scrolls through songs. Montana and Alana sit at a table and order mugs of beer. Ricky heads toward the bar. A BURLY BARTENDER named HORACE (43) greets him.

HORACE
You have some nerve showing your face around here, Ricky Six-Fingers.

RICKY
It's good to see you too, Horace. Get me a drink, will ya?

Horace fills a mug up and places it on the bar. Ricky drops some coins by it and takes a swig.

RICKY (CONT'D)
Put on a little weight since we've last talked, don't ya think?

Horace clenches his fists in anger.

RICKY (CONT'D)
I'm looking for Varnish. You seen him around here?

HORACE
He owns the place now.

RICKY
Oh, wow. Look at him go. I need to speak with him if you don't mind. He upstairs or something?

Two BODYGUARDS walk up behind Ricky.

Angry patrons and guards start to crowd around Montana and Alana. Piers is clueless.

HORACE
Here's what's gonna happen, pretty boy. You're gonna come outside with us and we're gonna smash your face in. Varnish sends his regards.

RICKY
Oh, does he? Alright, well, I have another idea. I'm gonna finish my drink-

Ricky chugs the rest of his drink.

RICKY (CONT'D)
And then we're gonna get this party started.

Ricky takes his mug and SHATTERS it on the head of one of the bodyguards. The other punches Ricky over the countertop.

As soon as this happens, a BAR FIGHT BREAKS OUT. It's complete chaos. Alana and Montana engage other patrons in brutal bare-knuckle BRAWLING, smashing chairs on people, punching them over tables, etc.

ALANA
Come on you scurvy seadogs!!

Piers realizes what's going on and selects a song on the jukebox.

PIERS
Okay, okay...fight music, fight music, fight music...

[Reference Song: 'Free Bird' by Lynyrd Skynyrd plays, starting at the guitar solo.]

PIERS (CONT'D)
YES! I've always wanted to get into a bar fight!

Piers gets tackled by a random patron. He squeals like a child.

The fight rages on as the bar explodes into chaos.

Alana gets PUNCHED over the bar countertop. She sees that Ricky is behind it too, still taking cover.

RICKY
Come here often?!

ALANA
This is your idea of a plan?!

RICKY
Isn't it amazing?!

ALANA
AYE!

RICKY
We need to get to the upstairs office. That's where my contact is!

ALANA
Got it!

Alana ROARS and leaps over the counter and joins the fight once again. Ricky follows.

Meanwhile, Piers is getting triple-teamed. Montana moves in and hits the attackers with the butt of his lever-action rifle. They're knocked unconscious.

PIERS
Thanks, Montana.

MONTANA
Don't mention it, Hoss!

Montana pulls him up, and they follow Alana and Ricky upstairs.

INT. NEO-TOKYO - VARNISH'S BAR - MANAGER'S OFFICE - NIGHT

Ricky kicks down the door to the manager's office, and a SHOTGUN BLAST nearly takes him out. It's VARNISH, (37) a cyborg rocker who's more robot than human. The heroes take cover.

RICKY
Long time no see, V!

VARNISH
Shut up, Ricky! You're trashing my bar!! Remember what I said if you showed your face around here again?

RICKY
Lemme guess. You'd shoot me?

CLICK. He's out. The heroes enter.

RICKY (CONT'D)
Nowhere to go, old man. Time to teach you a lesson about manners.

Varnish looks behind him and JUMPS out the window. Ricky sighs as he runs to the window and looks out into the alleyway. Varnish gets on one of two SPORTS BIKES and drives off.

ALANA
I thought you just needed to talk to him!

RICKY
(realizing)
Yeah, I do.
(beat)
That was a really poor choice of words, wasn't it?

ALANA
You idiot!

Ricky searches for an idea. Then-

Ricky LEAPS out the window. He gets on the other motorbike and starts it.

ALANA (CONT'D)
WHAT THE-

RICKY
Try and keep up!

He drives after Varnish. Piers looks around the room and finds an ION BOARD. He picks it up and turns it on.

PIERS
Can't be too different from longboarding.

ALANA
What?

PIERS
See you there!

Piers leaps out the window and sloppily rides the Ion Board, screaming with excitement as he does. Alana and Montana look at each other for a moment.

ALANA
Well, come on!!

They run downstairs.

EXT. NEO-TOKYO - NIGHT

The heroes all chase Varnish across the black & white, neon-drenched city. Ricky is on the sports bike, Piers is on the Ion Board, and Montana and Alana are on Domino.

The chase takes them through the streets of Neo-Tokyo as they all weave around flying cars, turn sharp corners, cross narrow light bridges, and leap over gaps, avoiding falling down a seemingly endless drop.

Eventually, Varnish goes up a ramp and lands on a GRAV-TRAIN. Ricky and Domino follow, barely making the jump. Piers hovers above.

Piers gets in close and leaps off the Ion Board, TACKLING Varnish onto a nearby METAL PLATFORM. Alana grabs the board as Domino and Ricky jump onto the platform, finally catching Varnish.

RICKY
Varnish!! Man, I just wanna talk!

VARNISH
You're crazy if you think I'm talking with you after what you just did!

RICKY
I get it, you're angry! But you don't gotta shoot me!!

VARNISH
Why are you even here?!

RICKY
I'm here to take Neo-Tokyo back from the Cyber-Samurai.

Varnish laughs.

VARNISH
Really? You and what army?

PIERS
Me.

Piers removes his cloak and mask, revealing his COLOR. Varnish looks at him in awe.

VARNISH
The creator. But you're just a child...

RICKY
See?

Varnish scans the area.

VARNISH
Follow me. We have to get back to my place before any cops show up.

INT. VARNISH'S APARTMENT - NIGHT

The heroes settle down in Varnish's place. Montana stares out the window, looking at the cyberpunk metropolis with his rifle ready.

Alana wraps Piers' wrist in BANDAGES after he hurt it tackling Varnish. Ricky talks to Varnish, who's lighting an e-cigarette.

VARNISH
Yeah, the whole city went belly up after you went solo. The Cyber-Samurai army marched in without a fight.

RICKY
Alright, buddy, don't act like I was the only thing stopping them from taking over. I'm just one guy.

VARNISH
Yeah, but after you left, the rest of the band split up. Cat gave up music.

Ricky flinches at the sound of Cat's name.

RICKY
She actually joined the rebellion?

Varnish nods.

RICKY (CONT'D)
Why didn't you?

VARNISH
I'm scared, Rick. The Cyber-Samurai aren't people you mess with. But that was the difference between her and us, wasn't it? She knew how to live for more.

Ricky paces around the room.

RICKY
(annoyed)
Oh, shut up. Just, shut up, okay? You're unbearable sometimes.

VARNISH
Ricky...

RICKY
(growing angry)
Where is Cat, V?

VARNISH
C'mon, Ricky. You knew what would happen when she joined. She's gone.

Ricky's hands shake. He laughs.

RICKY
(on the verge of tears)
She was so stupid, wasn't she? That girl... Oh man, Cat. You idiot...you stupid, stupid, idiot. She was always so...just...dumb!

In a sudden burst of anger, Ricky screams as he trashes the room. He grabs Piers and THROWS him against a wall.

RICKY (CONT'D)
I HATE YOU!! YOU ALLOWED THIS TO HAPPEN! YOU LET HER DIE!! I DIDN'T ASK FOR THIS! I DIDN'T ASK FOR CONFLICT! I DIDN'T ASK TO EXIST!! WHY WOULD YOU CREATE US IF YOU CAN'T EVEN FINISH THE JOB?! HAVE YOU EVER CONSIDERED THAT MAYBE YOU'RE NOT EVEN A GOOD WRITER?!!

Alana and Montana pull Ricky off. He falls over and sobs.

PIERS
(softly)
Ricky...I never wrote Cat. I never wrote any of this backstory. I only wrote you.

Ricky comes to a realization. He backs himself up against the wall.

RICKY
It's all my fault.

VARNISH
We have to fight for freedom, Rick. For Cat. We have to live for more.

This sinks in.

RICKY
How? They're unstoppable! We have nothing left!

PIERS
We have you, Ricky.

They all look at Piers.

PIERS (CONT'D)
We need to inspire revolution. We need to shake the people of the city out of apathy. What better than the return of the world's greatest rock star?

RICKY
I can't. I can't do it. I'm done with music.

PIERS
Ricky, please. Neo-Tokyo needs you. You're the only hope this city has left. It's what Cat would want.

RICKY
We can't play without her. She was the band's drummer.

PIERS
I can drum.

Ricky looks up at Piers. He gets up and goes into Varnish's bathroom.

INT. VARNISH'S APARTMENT - BATHROOM - NIGHT

Ricky closes the door to the bathroom and sits against the wall, breathing heavily. He takes out the PIECE OF PAPER and reads over it again.

He closes his eyes and takes a deep breath. Piers opens the door and closes it behind him.

RICKY
Go away, shrimp.

Piers sits down against the door and faces Ricky.

PIERS
What're you reading?

Ricky shakes his head.

RICKY
It's a letter Cat wrote me before I left.

PIERS
What's it say?

Ricky sighs.

RICKY
(brutally honest)
You really wanna know, kid? She tells me she loves me. She begs me to stay with her. She says that her life would be empty without me. I read it whenever I have to remind myself what I am...an arrogant, selfish, waste of space.

Piers listens intently. He moves close to Ricky.

PIERS
Or maybe it's a reminder of who you really are...someone who's loved by those closest to him...including me.

Ricky scoffs and gives a genuine smile.

RICKY
(endearingly)
Shut up, Piers.

Piers stands and holds his hand out to Ricky.

PIERS
What do you say, Rick? You in?

Ricky smirks and takes Piers' hand.

RICKY
I'm in.

INT. VARNISH'S APARTMENT - NIGHT

They return into the living room where everyone waits for them.

RICKY
It's time for Rock N' Roll to return to Neo-Tokyo.

The heroes cheer.

INT. VARNISH'S APARTMENT - NIGHT

The party of heroes stands around a table, a small holographic display in front of them.

[Reference Song: 'Fortunate Son' by Creedence Clearwater Revival plays.]

PIERS
Alright, if we're gonna pull this off, we're gonna need to do something big. Everyone in all of Neo-Tokyo needs to see it.

ALANA
How?

EXT. TANO MEDIA BUILDING - NIGHT

The party of heroes, now including Varnish, approaches the biggest skyscraper in all of Neo-Tokyo. They hold DUFFLE BAGS full of equipment. Piers now has the Ion Board carried on his back.

PIERS (V.O.)
All of Neo-Tokyo's broadcast systems are controlled by one company, all centralized in one building...the biggest in all of Neo-Tokyo...the Tano Media Building. I wrote a story about it once.

They avoid the main entrance and go around to a back alley where the maintenance entrance is.

PIERS (V.O.) (CONT'D)
If we can get to the roof of the building and set up a makeshift performance, we can live-stream it to the entire city.

RICKY (V.O.)
It's the most protected building in Neo-Tokyo. How do you expect us to get inside?

VARNISH (V.O.)
Horace has a second job in security there. He'll get us in through the back.

Horace opens a maintenance door for the party, letting them in.

INT. TANO MEDIA BUILDING - SERVICE HALLS - NIGHT

The party of heroes slinks through the service halls of the building, sneaking past guards, getting past cameras, and narrowly avoiding detection.

RICKY (V.O.)
Alright, shrimp, we're in. Then what?

PIERS (V.O.)
We'll split into two teams. Varnish, Ricky, Horace... you'll be with me. We'll go to the roof and set up the stage. Alana and Montana will head to the server room and disable the broadcast system's security.

Montana and Alana split off from Piers, Ricky, Varnish, and Horace. They go down separate halls that lead to different elevators.

INT. TANO MEDIA BUILDING - SERVER ROOM - NIGHT

Montana and Alana sneak into the server room. It's MASSIVE, holding access to every single one of the city's broadcast systems.

ALANA
(whispering)
You've gotta be kidding.

ALANA (V.O.)
What do we do when we get there?

Montana and Alana sneak through the room, avoiding guards.

PIERS (V.O.)
You have to find the master control panel and override their security systems using the instructions I'll give you. Once you do that, join us on the roof where we'll begin the live-stream.

Alana and Montana get to the MASTER CONTROL PANEL. It's complicated beyond belief.

Alana examines it. While she does, she takes a piece of crumbled-up paper out of her pocket and hands it to Montana.

ALANA
Here. Read me the instructions.

Montana examines them to no avail. The handwriting is comically atrocious.

MONTANA
(confused)
What in tarnation?

She looks at him, then snatches the paper from his hands and scans it, confused.

ALANA
You've gotta be kidding me.
(looking up at Montana)
20 years old. The lad's 20 years old.

She slowly follows his instructions while Montana keeps watch.

EXT. TANO MEDIA BUILDING - ROOF - NIGHT

Ricky, Varnish, Horace, and Piers wait for the go-ahead to start. The stage is nearly set up. Piers nervously paces. Horace stands by a control tower where a panel is open, waiting to plug the camera in.

PIERS
(to himself)
What's taking them so long?
(into comms)
Alana, we're running out of time.

ALANA (O.S.)
Well, maybe if you didn't write like a child, I would get this done faster.

Piers sighs in frustration. But then-

HORACE
We're ready to go!

Ricky, Varnish, and Piers get into positions.

VARNISH (V.O.)
Do you realize what we're doing? After we pull this off, there's no more hiding. The Shadow and the Cyber-Samurai will come after you with full force. You're going to war, Piers. Are you ready for that?

Piers finishes setting up the drums. Ricky looks back at him.

RICKY
You sure you can play with that bandage on?

PIERS
Come on, Ricky. I could play blindfolded with one arm!

RICKY
Here, take these.

Ricky tosses a pair of TAPED DRUMSTICKS.

PIERS
What are they?

RICKY
They were Cat's drumsticks. They're yours now.
(strumming power chords)
On my queue, shrimp.

Piers nods as he TWIRLS the drumsticks.

PIERS (V.O.)
I know exactly what this is...which is why I know it's gonna work.

Horace gives them the thumbs up.

PIERS
You ready, man?

Ricky looks back and gives Piers a devilish smile.

RICKY
I'm no man, kid. I'm DYNAMITE.

[Reference Song: 'The Pretender' by Foo Fighters plays.]

EXT. NEO-TOKYO - NIGHT

The song begins.

The band appears on screens across the city. The denizens of Neo-Tokyo come out of their homes and closed businesses to witness the event.

An unstoppable energy flows through citizens all over. Crowds form around unsettled Cyber-Samurai checkpoints and patrols.

INT. BLACK BANDIT'S SHIP - NIGHT

Black Bandit flies her ship through Neo-Tokyo as they see the broadcast. She walks into the cockpit with the pilots.

BLACK BANDIT
Stop.

The ship stops in front of a GIANT SCREEN broadcasting the band.

BLACK BANDIT (CONT'D)
No!

She leaves the cockpit and arms up.

BLACK BANDIT (CONT'D)
I want all available Cyber-Samurai ships to converge on the roof of the Tano Media Building ASAP!! We have to stop that performance!!

Her ship flies up through the skies of Neo-Tokyo, followed by a growing SQUADRON of Cyber-Samurai attack ships.

INT. TANO MEDIA BUILDING - SERVER ROOM - NIGHT

Montana and Alana sprint through the server room when-

RED LIGHTS begin to flash. The building goes on full alert. LASER FIRE rips past them as their position is compromised.

They bob and weave past the server blocks, dodging fire from armored guards.

Alana leads Montana as he brandishes his lever-action and fires back.

ALANA
Come on!

As they run, METAL BARRIERS slam down on the doors, blocking their only exit out. They stop.

MONTANA
Shoot!

Alana screams and runs toward the metal barrier. She shoulder checks it and BREAKS through the metal. Montana stands in utter shock.

ALANA
Come on, Montana! The roof!

MONTANA
Yes, ma'am!

Montana catches up with her and they run down the halls.

EXT. TANO MEDIA BUILDING - ROOF - NIGHT

Horace runs over to his duffel bag and unzips it, revealing a huge LASER CANNON.

As this happens, Cyber-Samurai ships fly up to the roof and face the band. They're about to fire on them when-

Horace fires the laser cannon at the leading ship, blowing a huge hole in it. The ship drops to the side and takes out another ship. They both explode.

Other ships come from the side and Cyber-Samurai drop down. As this happens, Horace picks up a GATLING LASER from another bag and unleashes laser fire, attempting to hold them off.

EXT. NEO-TOKYO - NIGHT

With screens broadcasting the battle on the roof, the denizens of Neo-Tokyo FIGHT back against their Cyber-Samurai oppressors in mobs, destroying property, going through checkpoints, and overwhelming guards.

THE REVOLUTION BEGINS.

EXT. TANO MEDIA BUILDING - ROOF - NIGHT

The band plays in full focus. Ricky goes into an epic improvised GUITAR SOLO, shredding like nobody has before with his six metal fingers.

But as he does, Black Bandit's ship arrives on the scene. The side of the ship opens up and a Cyber-Samurai soldier using a laser turret rains down fire on the band. Ricky and Varnish leap out of the way as they still play.

BLACK BANDIT
STOP! THAT! SONG!!!! NOW!!!!

Black Bandit pushes the man arming the turret out of the way.

BLACK BANDIT (CONT'D)
Out of my way!

She takes a LASER LEVER-ACTION RIFLE and aims it straight at Piers, the only stationary member.

BLACK BANDIT (CONT'D)
Time to die, Piers!!

But then-

Montana hits her rifle with a pistol shot. Alana leaps into the fray with Horace and tries to hold off the waves of oncoming Cyber-Samurai.

The song reaches an EPIC CLIMAX as Montana, Alana, and Horace fight back against Cyber-Samurai, protecting the greatest rock concert in the world.

Piers then breaks out into an epic drum solo, completely lost in the moment.

As his solo comes to a close, Piers leaves the drum set and goes to the middle of the stage.

He kneels and puts his hand down. COLOR slowly emits from the ground below him.

Black Bandit's ship lands on the roof. She beelines for the stage, but Montana LASSOS her and pulls her back. She takes a knife out and CUTS the rope.

BLACK BANDIT (CONT'D)
I'm not here for you, Montana. I'm here for Piers!

MONTANA
It's not too late to come back. I know there's still good in you.

BLACK BANDIT
Shut up! I'm ending this!

MONTANA
Abigail, please!!

As soon as he says that, Bandit's rage overtakes her.

ABIGAIL
I said shut up!!

She spins and whips out her laser pistol. Montana reaches for his six-shooter. But he's too late. She BLASTS Montana, and laser fire goes straight through his shooting hand.

ALANA
NO!!!!

Alana ragefully RIPS through Cyber-Samurai as she makes her way toward Montana. Horace follows her.

Abigail walks toward a downed Montana and points her gun at him. But Alana leaps and KICKS her back, sending her sliding across the ground.

Varnish and Ricky keep playing. Abigail rises and points her gun at Alana, ready to shoot, but then-

The color around Abigail is restored. For a second, ALL FIGHTING STOPS.

Everyone is amazed as color is returned to all of Neo-Tokyo. The colorful glowing neon lights shine in the darkness. After it's over, Piers once again passes out.

Seeing this as their ticket out, the party of heroes books it to the exit off the roof. Ricky clips the drumsticks to Piers' jeans and carries him out.

As the dust settles, Abigail walks to the edge of the building and looks out at the city. Barely noticeable TEARS fall down her cheeks.

ABIGAIL
What are you waiting for?! After them!

But the Cyber-Samurai all drop their weapons and sit down, staring at the color in the night sky.

INT. TANO MEDIA BUILDING - ELEVATOR - NIGHT

The heroes run down a hallway and crowd into an elevator. As it descends, they all COLLAPSE, exhausted. Piers slowly comes to.

PIERS
Did we win?

RICKY
I know one thing for sure. That was the best solo this town has ever heard.

Slowly, they all begin to laugh, half out of relief, half out of fear.

ALANA
You realize that when we step out those doors, an entire army of Cyber-Samurai is gonna be waiting for us?

RICKY
Well, let's give em one last show, even if they take us down with them.

PIERS
Together?

They all nod.

RICKY
Together.

The elevator reaches the lower floors. They all get up and prepare to fight.

INT. NEO-TOKYO - TANO MEDIA BUILDING - LOBBY - NIGHT

DING!

As the elevator opens, they all let out war cries and jump into the lobby.

But the Cyber-Samurai don't do anything.

They sit and stare at the color of the lobby, letting the heroes cautiously pass.

PIERS
No shot.

They walk out of the lobby and into the street without a fight.

EXT. TANO MEDIA BUILDING - ENTRANCE

When they reach the outdoors, a crowd of rioters CHEERS for them.

PIERS
So this is what it feels like.

RICKY
What?

PIERS
To be a rock star.

They stand triumphant.

EXT. VARNISH'S APARTMENT - NIGHT

Alana, Piers, and Montana pack their stuff up on Domino. Ricky talks with Varnish and Horace.

RICKY
You sure you boys can't come with? We could use the muscle.

VARNISH
Our city needs us, Rick. Just like the kid needs you.

RICKY
Alright, well don't try and shoot next time I come back for a drink.

VARNISH
(winking)
No promises.

They hug.

Piers comes up, holding the Ion Board.

PIERS
Sorry I kind of stole it.

VARNISH
Keep it, Piers. It's yours now.

Piers smiles and shakes Varnish's hand.

PIERS
Thanks, Varnish. I owe you one.

VARNISH
If you need me, you know where to find me.

ALANA
Ahoy, lads! We don't got all night!

The heroes leave. Varnish takes a long drag from an e-cigarette.

VARNISH
I need a drink.

As they walk away, Ricky pulls Piers in and tousles his hair like an older brother would.

RICKY
Wow, look at you, tough guy! Slick new Ion Board, new drum sticks, and now you're a rock star. How you feeling?

PIERS
I'm okay, I guess.

RICKY
Oh, come on! What? You're a hero, man!

PIERS
Eh...I'm just me.

Ricky gives him a look of confusion, then pulls him along with the group.

EXT. NEO-TOKYO OUTSKIRTS - NIGHT

The heroes ride out across the fields outside of Neo-Tokyo. In the distance, they can see the city lights lit up in glorious color. FIREWORKS dance across the sky to celebrate their liberation.

A ship tails them from a distance. It's Abigail.

ABIGAIL
All available Cyber-Samurai units, converge on my location, now! We have to stop them from liberating Keda!!

EXT. THE WILDERNESS - DAY/NIGHT

MONTAGE:

The party of heroes journey across extensive wilderness, once again encountering strange creatures, formations, and landscapes until they reach BLACK AND WHITE territory again.

EXT. THE FORESTS OF KEDA - DAY

The heroes rest at another makeshift campsite. Montana plays Five Finger Fillet. Alana and Piers are practicing sword fighting.

PIERS
You know, I'm starting to get the feeling that sword fighting might not be my thing.

ALANA
You'll get the hang of it eventually. Just believe in yourself.

PIERS
Yeah, I'm not so sure it's that simple.

All of a sudden, Piers loses his balance, nearly fainting. Alana catches him.

ALANA
Woah, woah! Piers, are you okay?

PIERS
Yeah...I'm just...exhausted.

Ricky speaks with a holographic Cerra.

CERRA
Are the rumors true? Did the legendary Ricky Six-Fingers make his glorious return to Rock N Roll?

RICKY
Heck yeah, he did. I wish you could've seen it, Cerr. It was amazing.

CERRA
Well, good. Now ye can finally put that empty concert venue in the ship to good use.

RICKY
We can have a celebration concert when we get back.

CERRA
I'm looking forward to it, lad. Ye play good music. I'm glad you're doing it again.

RICKY
Yeah, well don't tell him I said this, but I couldn't have done it without the kid.

CERRA
(winking)
Your secret's safe with me. Go save Keda, lad.

RICKY
Yes ma'am.

Ricky hangs up and joins Montana.

RICKY (CONT'D)
You ready to get your butt kicked again, cowboy?

MONTANA
(suddenly alert)
Ricky, stop.

RICKY
You kidding me, Tex? When I'm on a hot streak like this?

MONTANA
Ricky!

Montana tackles Ricky and covers his mouth.

MONTANA (CONT'D)
Everyone, hush!

In the distance, the engine of a ship can be heard. Then-

PIERS
RUN!

EXPLOSIONS rock the trees around them as a Cyber-Samurai attack ship makes a run through their camp. The group is in disarray as they're knocked back by the shockwaves.

ALANA
It's coming back around!

Montana fires at the ship with his left hand. He MISSES every shot. His shooting hand is useless.

When Piers recovers, he goes for his Ion Board. He kicks it up and steps on it, hovering above the ground.

MONTANA
Piers! Catch!

Montana throws his six-shooter, and Piers catches it. The ship comes back around for another run. Piers aims down the sight.

PIERS
Come on, come on, you got this, Piers. You got this!

Piers FIRES and HITS the window of the ship. It flies off to the side and explodes in the trees.

PIERS (CONT'D)
HA! You see that?!

MONTANA
Mighty fine shootin, kid, but we gotta git!

Montana picks up an unconscious Ricky and puts him on the back of Domino.

A TRIO of ships appears in an opening of destroyed trees.

It's Abigail.

ABIGAIL
(desperately)
You're mine!!

The ships zoom toward them.

PIERS
Uh oh.

MONTANA
Follow me! Yah!

Domino gallops off.

PIERS
Alana!

Piers reaches out his hand. Alana leaps up and catches it. She pulls herself onto the back of his Ion Board.

PIERS (CONT'D)
Nice catch!

ALANA
Eyes on the road, lad!

Piers narrowly misses a tree. The chase rages on through the forests as the ships fire down upon Domino and the Ion Board. Ricky slowly wakes up.

RICKY
Wh...What's going on?

He realizes what's happening.

RICKY (CONT'D)
WHAT THE...Oh, of course, I get knocked out for one second and everything falls apart!

MONTANA
Hush up and hold on!

The attack ships DESTROY everything in their path as they try and fire on the heroes. An increasingly desperate Abigail screams in rage as she burns down the forests.

But the forests are too dense. She loses them.

ABIGAIL
Where are you?!

SHADOW APPEARS in a hologram on her ship, startling her.

SHADOW
You're failing me.

ABIGAIL
What are you doing?! I'm the one out here every day chasing them!

A holographic Storm-Reaper slithers up to her.

SHADOW
I'm preparing the Catalyst, bandit. But obviously, since you lack the competence to carry out this mission, I will have to do it myself.

ABIGAIL
Will you meet me in Keda?

SHADOW
No. Like the rest of their adventures, Keda is just a distraction. I will strike at their heart.

Shadow hangs up. Abigail SMASHES her dashboard in frustration.

ABIGAIL
I won't be a failure. I am NOT a failure.

EXT. THE FORESTS OF KEDA - WOLF-PACK TERRITORY - DAY

The heroes ride through the forest.

PIERS
I think we lost them.

RICKY
HA! That'll teach them to mess with-

Montana and Ricky hit a WIRE in the trees, knocking them off Domino.

ALANA
What the-

A rope wraps around Piers and he's pulled up into the forest. Alana falls off the board, landing in the brush below. She brandishes her sword.

She hears shuffling in the woods. Then-

A HOWL. A rope wraps around her foot. She's pulled into the forest.

INT. WOLF-PACK HIDEOUT - TIMEOUT ROOM - DAY

Darkness.

Then- a LANTERN lights up.

Piers and Ricky are tied up to chairs back-to-back. They see a pack of children wearing furs and staring at them.

FINLAY (15) stands in front of them in his wolf costume. There's mud slathered on his face and a crazed look in his eye. He speaks with an unthreatening nasally voice and unquenchable energy.

FINLAY
You better start talking, rainbow boy!

Ricky laughs uncontrollably.

PIERS
What?

RICKY
I think it's past your bedtime, junior.

He punches Ricky in the stomach.

FINLAY
How about I cut your hair with my teeth? You look like a girl.

But then, BONNIE, (16) the leader of the group of children, steps into the room. She's strong-willed, charismatic, and determined.

BONNIE
Wolf-Pack!

The children step into attention and let out a little growl.

BONNIE (CONT'D)
Finlay, keeping our guests comfortable?

FINLAY
Yes, ma'am.

RICKY
Oh, far from it. I've seen better service from-

PIERS
Ricky, enough!

BONNIE
(to Piers)
Are you his boss?

PIERS
(cheeky)
Yeah, something like that.

RICKY
Why you little-

Finlay punches Ricky again.

PIERS
What's your name?

BONNIE
I'm Bonnie. We're the Wolf-Pack.

PIERS
Hey, Bonnie. I'm Piers. I'm the creator.

The children look at each other for a second.

FINLAY
What's a creator?

Bonnie shrugs.

BONNIE
What were you doing with Mr. Smith?!

RICKY
(beyond annoyed)
Oh, brother! That's what this is about?

A WOLF-PACK GUARD enters the room.

WOLF-PACK GUARD
Hey, Boss! Mr. Smith just woke up! He says they're with him!

BONNIE
Oh.

RICKY
HA! That's right, you little twerp! Now get these ropes off me before I-

Finlay fake-out punches Ricky, who squirms back.

FINLAY
(chuckling)
Gotcha.

INT. WOLF-PACK HIDEOUT - MAIN AREA - DAY

Bonnie and Finlay escort the heroes through the hideout, an underground VILLAGE consisting of entirely children.

BONNIE
Gentlemen...welcome to the Wolf-Pack, Keda's best freedom fighters.

PIERS
I don't remember writing this.

RICKY
I hate kids.

PIERS
Hey, play nice.

They walk to the middle of the village. Montana and Alana go over battle strategies with the children.

RICKY
Alright, cowboy, you better have a good explanation for what's going on.

A Wolf-Pack CHILD steps in front of Ricky, blocking him off. Ricky sighs, palms the child, and pushes him to the side.

RICKY (CONT'D)
Montana!

CHILD
His name is Mr. Smith!

Ricky looks like he's about to explode.

RICKY
Someone hold me back right now or I'm gonna take a swing.

ALANA
(whistling)
Ricky!

Ricky runs to Alana and takes cover behind her.

PIERS
(confused)
Mr. Smith, what's going on?

MONTANA
(distracted)
Hmm?

Piers leans in.

PIERS
I never wrote a Wolf-Pack. Keda is supposed to have...you know...minotaurs and fairies and gremlins and halflings and treants and stuff like that. Where are they?

MONTANA
They're here.

Montana slides a HAND-DRAWN MAP across the table to Piers. He looks over it for a second. It's complicated beyond belief.

PIERS
Right...well I have no idea how to read maps so this simply does nothing for me.

MONTANA
It's a Cyber-Samurai prison. It's where they keep all the creatures of Keda.

BONNIE
And with Mr. Smith's help, we're gonna break them out! We've been planning this for weeks!
(to Montana)
I'm sorry again about hurting you earlier. I didn't know that-

MONTANA
Bonnie, that's enough apologizin' out of you.

PIERS
So, that's it? We go and stage a prison break? You know the Black Bandit is gonna be there, right? No tragic backstory or blinding insecurities I should know about?

MONTANA
(matter of fact)
No.

ALANA
Aye! Let's get this show on the road.

INT. WOLF-PACK HIDEOUT - WEAPONS ROOM - DAY

Finlay shows Piers all the weapons they have.

FINLAY
And this one is a rock spear, and this one is a rock sword, and this one is...well, just a rock.

PIERS
You guys sure like your rocks.

FINLAY
Yes, we do!

A WOLF HOWL echoes in the distance.

FINLAY (CONT'D)
OH! Gotta go, Piers. I'll see you on the surface!

Finlay leaves. Soon after, Ricky, Alana, and Montana enter the room. They're all geared up and ready to go.

PIERS
So this is it, huh? Hard to believe it's almost over.
(laughs)
It's been a crazy few weeks.

ALANA
Hey, we can do this. You can do this.

Alana leaves.

RICKY
Yeah, as much as I can't stand these kids, it's gonna feel good to be a hero.

Ricky leaves.

Piers looks at Montana. The cowboy clears his throat.

PIERS
What's going on, Montana? How do these kids know you? Why do they treat you like a king? And why did you leave them?

MONTANA
That's enough out of you.

PIERS
Alana told me everything about her, and I was able to help Ricky. I wanna be here for you.

MONTANA
I ain't the one that needs help. Them kids do. So let's focus on them, then you can talk to me.

PIERS
Everyone needs someone to talk to, Montana. Even someone as cool as you.

Montana nods and leaves.

PIERS (CONT'D)
(to himself)
Alright, let's rock and roll.

EXT. THE FORESTS OF KEDA - DAY

[Reference Song: 'Thunderstruck' by AC/DC plays.]

The heroes and the Wolf-Pack gather in the forests. Ricky is unimpressed by the supposed child freedom fighters.

RICKY
So what, this is it? A bunch of kids with sticks and leaves on their backs?

BONNIE
Nah, watch this. Hit it, Finlay.

Finlay blows a horn that echoes through the wilderness. Soon after, the entire tribe joins in, howling like crazy.

The heroes look at each other. Montana takes off his hat and howls first. Piers and Alana follow. Ricky chuckles, sighs, then lets out one of his own.

As soon as he does, A GIANT WOLF leaps off a rock and over him. Bonnie jumps on top of it and grabs onto its fur. She brandishes her ROCK SPEAR, holding it in the air.

BONNIE (CONT'D)
Wolf-Pack!! Let's ride!!

PIERS
(laughing)
No shot.

EXT. CYBER-SAMURAI PRISON - DAY

Guards patrol the prison walls overlooking the forest expanse. Everything is quiet until-

THE HOWL.

Bonnie, Ricky, Montana, and the rest of the Wolf-Pack ride on the Cyber-Samurai prison, the children all howling like mad. The sudden assault surprises the prison guards. They fire at the heroes.

BONNIE
For Keda!!

The wolves dodge LASER FIRE, bobbing and weaving between trees, using the dense forests as cover.

Bonnie lights a stick of DYNAMITE, places it on a slingshot, and fires it at the walls of the prison.

BOOM!

The explosion reduces the wall to rubble. Another howl. The assault rages on as the Cyber-Samurai guards gather to defend.

EXT. CYBER-SAMURAI PRISON - BACKSIDE - DAY

On the other side of the prison, Piers, Alana, and Finlay climb up the walls, the crazed child warrior leading them.

PIERS
(to Alana)
I think this kid's got a screw loose or something.

ALANA
Isn't it amazing?

PIERS
Oh yeah.

EXT. CYBER-SAMURAI PRISON - MAIN COURTYARD - DAY

As the main assault spills into the courtyard, the trio sneaks around. Any guards that come into contact with them are easily taken care of by a bloodthirsty Finlay.

Wolf-Pack numbers are dwindling quickly.

INT. CYBER-SAMURAI PRISON - DAY

The trio sneaks through the inside of the prison. It's retro-futuristic and industrial, neon gears and chains churning out steam and smoke. Alarms blare as Cyber-Samurai troops run past the sneaking heroes.

PIERS
We need to hurry. We're running out of time.

FINLAY
Try and keep up, butt-head.

Finlay runs ahead, giggling.

ALANA
(cheeky)
You heard the man.

PIERS
(smiling)
Oh, did I?

They follow.

EXT. CYBER-SAMURAI PRISON - MAIN COURTYARD - DAY

The Wolf-Pack uses guerilla tactics against the Cyber-Samurai: jumping from trees, hiding in the woods, etc. But then-

SHIP ENGINES ROAR up above. Montana looks at the sky in horror.

A HUGE CYBER-SAMURAI CRUISER flies above them.

MONTANA
Oh no.

RICKY
What?!

MONTANA
Reinforcements.

The ship fires down on the Wolf-Pack. The heroes are hopelessly outmatched.

INT. CYBER-SAMURAI PRISON - THE PIT - DAY

They find their way to the cell blocks. Massive walls of prison cages for varying creatures are connected by catwalks on different levels. It's all above a seemingly endless drop into darkness.

In the middle of the huge opening is a circular platform where the WARDEN stands. He chants to the creatures.

WARDEN
THERE IS NO POINT. THERE IS NO FIGHT. THERE IS NO FIRE.

The Warden, standing over SEVEN FEET tall, repeats this over and over again.

Piers falls to his knees in shock.

PIERS
Oh no...

The Warden sees them and growls, brandishing a huge TWO SIDED BLADE. Alana picks Piers up.

ALANA
Piers, Finlay, you free the creatures. I'll take the big guy.

FINLAY
You kidding me, woman? I want in on this dance.

ALANA
(chuckling)
You got it, kid. Let's kick his butt.

Finlay howls as he runs down a catwalk, charging the Warden. Alana follows, howling after him. Piers charges up his Ion Board and flies to a random cell.

The duo engages the Warden on the catwalks. Alana fights with her sword, and Finlay fights with his rock staff.

It's immediately obvious how powerful the Warden is as he knocks them around like ragdolls. He THROWS Finlay off the catwalk and onto a lower level. Alana is losing.

Piers stands at a cell, but he's surprised when he notices that nothing holds the creatures in. No door, no bars...nothing. He looks inside. A small FAIRY sits.

PIERS
I don't understand. Why don't you all just leave? We're here to rescue you!

FAIRY
There's no point. There's no point in anything. There's nothing left out there for us.

PIERS
What?

FAIRY
I want to leave, but my legs can't move. I want to live, but there's no life on the outside.

Piers takes this in.

The fight with the Warden continues as they battle across multiple levels of catwalks. Alana fights with skill and prowess, while Finlay fights with an enraged passion.

ALANA
Piers!!

He turns to see Alana and Finlay getting pummeled by the Warden.

ALANA (CONT'D)
If you could hurry, that'd be great!

Piers looks at the circular platform in the middle, then sparks an idea. He gets on his board and rides to it.

PIERS
(to himself)
Man, I'm so tired.

He prepares to give a rousing, heroic speech. The Fairy watches from the corner of her cell.

PIERS (CONT'D)
You all know who I am. And I bet you’re frustrated. I bet you’re angry. I bet you're-

A sharp pain splits through his body. He ignores it and continues.

PIERS (CONT'D)
I bet you wonder why you're-

It hits him again, and he falls to his knees. A dark energy force surrounds Piers and separates him from the material world.

Alana sees this black energy surround him. She is helpless to stop it. She battles the Warden, losing badly.

ALANA
Piers!!

SHADOW APPEARS.

SHADOW
You thought you could give one heroic speech and save the day?

PIERS
(in intense pain)
Yeah, kind of.

The Storm-Reaper slithers around Piers' neck. It suffocates him.

SHADOW
Call out to them, Piers! They won't save you. Nothing can! You've already lost!

Piers resists Shadow and crawls toward the cells. He reaches his hand out and opens the dark energy field so the Fairy can see him.

PIERS
Please!! Help!! The world needs you!! I need you!!

The Fairy stands and walks to the edge of the cell. She and Piers lock eyes.

PIERS (CONT'D)
Have faith!! Fight!! Light the fire and fight!! It's the only...way...

Piers uses all of his energy to reach out to the Fairy.

PIERS (CONT'D)
(dying)
Please...I need you...

A look of determination washes across her face.

EXT. CYBER-SAMURAI PRISON - MAIN COURTYARD - DAY

Ricky, Bonnie, Montana, and the rest are slowly surrounded by Cyber-Samurai. They fight a desperate battle for survival.

BONNIE
Don't surrender!!

A LASER hits Bonnie's Wolf. She falls off, incapacitated.

More laser fire rains down from above, taking out scores of Wolf-Pack members. It's Abigail's ship.

As it lands, the Cyber-Samurai completely surround the remaining heroes. They all drop their weapons. Abigail pushes her way through the Cyber-Samurai, brandishing her laser pistol.

ABIGAIL
Finally! I have you right where I want you! Where's Piers?!

MONTANA
He ain't here, Abigail. He's long gone.

RICKY
Wait. Her name isn't Black Bandit?

MONTANA
Hush!

ABIGAIL
You expect me to believe that, old man?

Abigail looks around. She spots Bonnie.

ABIGAIL (CONT'D)
Give me Bonnie!

MONTANA
No!

Montana runs, but Abigail shoots the ground around him. He can't move. Cyber-Samurai give a squirming Bonnie to Abigail. She holds a laser pistol to her head.

ABIGAIL
Tell me where he is, or little Bonnie here gets it!

MONTANA
Abigail, please! Don't do this!

ABIGAIL
Shut up! I'll do it!

MONTANA
Abigail...

She looks at Montana, tears welling in her eyes.

ABIGAIL
I can't fail. I have to do this.

But then, the ground rumbles, and-

The WARDEN'S HELMET bursts out of the ground and lands in front of Abigail. She looks down in confusion.

ABIGAIL (CONT'D)
What the-

A GIANT TREE HAND PUNCHES THROUGH THE GROUND, AND A HUGE TREE GIANT CLIMBS OUT. IT LETS OUT A HORN-LIKE CALL OF THE WILD.

Scores of mythical creatures climb up and into their home, attacking the Cyber-Samurai. The Fairy flies Piers into the middle of the courtyard.

The battle rages as the mythical creatures and the heroes push back. They're winning.

Abigail falls over and drops her laser pistol. Montana and Abigail lock eyes and make a break for the weapon. But then-

BOOM!

The Tree Giant's foot SLAMS down. They both climb onto the branches, making their way up the Tree Giant's body until they get to the top of the head.

EXT. TREE GIANT'S HEAD - DAY

As soon as they both get on top of the head, Abigail charges Montana with her knife. They clash. Because of Montana's busted hand, Abigail easily bests the old cowboy. She pins him down, her knife against his throat.

ABIGAIL
You can't beat me, Montana!!

MONTANA
Which is why I'm done fightin' you.

A moment passes. Abigail screams, throws the knife away, and stumbles back.

ABIGAIL
You were supposed to protect me.
You were supposed to keep me safe!

MONTANA
(desperate)
I tried! You were like a daughter
to me. I loved you.

ABIGAIL
Then why'd you let Shadow take me
from you?!

Nothing.

ABIGAIL (CONT'D)
TALK, MONTANA! FOR ONCE IN YOUR LIFE, SAY SOMETHING!!!

Montana sheds his first tears.

MONTANA
Because I'm weak. I ain't a man. I'm a coward. It's my fault it took you from me. It's my fault the Cyber-Samurai took over Keda. I was supposed to protect the forest. I was supposed to protect you! But I failed. And I haven't been able to live with myself since. A day don't go by where I don't think of what happened.

ABIGAIL
You don't know what it's like to be given up on. You don't know what it's like to be forgotten about. To be treated like nobody notices. To be a failure!

MONTANA
(pleading)
Yes, I do, because I am a failure. I have failed you. Can't you see what it's put me through, Abby?! Can't you see what it's done to me?! Please, come back to the light. I can't live like this!

ABIGAIL
Then let me put you out of your misery.

But before Abigail can finish Montana, laser fire hits the Tree Giant in the shoulder, stumbling it. Montana slides off the head, holding onto the edge with one hand. Abigail stands above him.

ABIGAIL (CONT'D)
Goodbye, Montana.

MONTANA
(determined)
If dyin' is the only way you can feel whole again, then I'm willin' to do my duty.

Abigail and Montana LOCK EYES, Abigail deeply struggling.

Then, Montana's grip slips and he falls.

But Abigail dives forward and CATCHES his hand, holding onto him. She screams as she pulls him up and back onto the head. When she does, she hugs him, sobbing.

ABIGAIL
I'm sorry. I'm so sorry.

MONTANA
I am too, Abby.

EXT. CYBER-SAMURAI PRISON - MAIN COURTYARD - DAY

When the fight ends, the heroes stand in the courtyard. They're exhausted from the battle.

After a few moments, Montana and Abigail climb down the Tree Giant and join the rest. As soon as they spot Abigail, they all point their weapons at her.

MONTANA
Hey! She's with us now!

RICKY
You kidding me?! She's been chasing us down this whole time! She was gonna kill Bonnie!

They all look at an exhausted Bonnie. She makes eye contact with Abigail.

BONNIE
If Montana trusts her, so does the Wolf-Pack. It's good to have you back, Abigail.

Ricky looks around, confused.

RICKY
So does everyone just KNOW each other now?!

While this happens, Piers kneels down and gives color back to the world.

The forests of Keda and the natural wilderness beyond are all re-colored. Nature teems with life once again.

Piers collapses into Alana again, this last one taking all of his energy.

The creatures of Keda and the Wolf-Pack celebrate. They cheer, yell, and howl like crazy.

BONNIE
Thanks for everything, Montana. We couldn't have done this without you.

MONTANA
Thanks, Bonnie. It feels good to be home again.

They hug. Finlay timidly approaches Alana.

FINLAY
(sincerely)
It was really nice fighting with you.

ALANA
Thanks, Finlay. We make a good team.

Finlay blushes. He hugs Alana, taking her by surprise. After celebrating, the heroes, and now Abigail, reconvene around Alana and Piers, who slowly comes to.

Montana pulls Piers up and hugs him tightly.

MONTANA
You saved us, Hoss. I owe you my life.

PIERS
I didn't do anything, Montana.

MONTANA
You feeling alright?

PIERS
Yeah, I'll be okay.

Montana pulls him in close again, hugging him like a father would.

ALANA
What now?

RICKY
We can finally go home and see Cerra.

They all smile in a sweet moment of relief. Ricky drops down his holo-pad to call her. They all wait for Cerra to pick up. But nobody answers.

Ricky tries again. Nothing. He tries again. Nothing. Fear spreads among the group.

RICKY (CONT'D)
What's happening? What's going on? Why isn't she picking up?!

Then, Abigail remembers. The Shadow APPEARS, pacing around the group. Only Piers can see it. His eyes go wide.

ABIGAIL
Oh no.

Ricky's eyes dart toward Abigail. He sprints to her and SLAMS her on the ground.

RICKY
(enraged)
WHAT DID YOU DO?!

As the heroes pull Ricky off Abigail, Shadow goes in close to Piers.

SHADOW
Tell them what you know to be true.

The tension is unbearable.

PIERS
The Shadow.

They all look at Piers. Tears well in Ricky's eyes. Abigail and Piers make eye contact.

PIERS (CONT'D)
We took too long. The Shadow is at the Odessa.

EXT. CYBER-SAMURAI PRISON - MAIN COURTYARD - DAY

Abigail's dropship lifts off the ground and zooms into the sky. The Wolf-Pack looks up as they fly off. Bonnie pets Domino, who Montana left with her.

INT. ABIGAIL'S SHIP - DAY

Abigail pilots the dropship with Montana. Piers sits in the back with his head in his hands. Shadow stands over him, mocking him. Ricky paces around, fuming.

RICKY
I KNEW WE SHOULDN'T HAVE LEFT! I KNEW IT!!
(to Piers)
THIS IS ALL YOUR FAULT!!

ALANA
RICKY! STOP! Calm down!

RICKY
CALM DOWN?! HOW AM I SUPPOSED TO BE CALM WHEN-

The darkness surrounds Piers again.

SHADOW
Your fault. It's all YOUR fault.

Piers screams and cries, but no sounds come out. Shadow wraps its hand around Piers' throat, pushing him further into the darkness. He falls deeper and deeper, screaming and yelling as if he's being pulled underwater.

ALANA
Piers!!

Piers looks up at a concerned Alana. His face drips with sweat. He shakes.

PIERS
Alana...I can't.

Laser fire rocks the ship.

ABIGAIL
Hold on tight, everyone!! We're going in hot!!

Alana carries Piers to the front of the ship.

The Odessa is on fire. Cyber-Samurai ships rip it apart. They're barreling right towards it. Another shot hits the ship. The heroes are THROWN around.

ABIGAIL (CONT'D)
BRACE FOR IMPACT!!

Piers closes his eyes and holds his hands over his ears. He screams.

INT. THE ODESSA - DAY

Piers wakes up in CHAOS. The ship is in ruins. Pirates run in fear as Cyber-Samurai board the Odessa, KILLING all of them. He stands and stumbles around.

The other heroes slowly crawl out of the wreckage.

ALANA
We need to get to the bridge! Now!

PIERS
This was a trap! I can feel it.
It's here to kill me.

ALANA
I won't let that happen. Come on!!

Alana carries Piers across the ship. The heroes protect him as they claw through groups of Cyber-Samurai on their way to the bridge.

INT. THE ODESSA - BRIDGE - DAY

The heroes make it to the bridge where they find Cerra struggling to hold off a group of Cyber-Samurai with her cutlass and a laser hand cannon.

CERRA
Come on, you bilge rats! That's all
you got?!

RICKY
CERRA!

Ricky leaps into action to fight the Cyber-Samurai. The heroes join him.

They defeat the Cyber-Samurai. Ricky hugs Cerra.

RICKY (CONT'D)
I thought you were dead!

CERRA
It takes more than that to kill me,
boyo.

RICKY
We never should've left you.

CERRA
I knew the sacrifice I would have to make.

She looks at Piers. Her expression turns to FEAR.

CERRA (CONT'D)
(to Piers)
Ye shouldn't be here. Ye need to leave, NOW!

RICKY
Cerra, we weren't just going to leave you behind!

CERRA
You should've.

PIERS
How do we get out?

CERRA
The hangar. There might be some dropships left for us to-

Abigail sees something.

ABIGAIL
WATCH OUT!

They all look at the decaying glass panels on the other side of the bridge as a MISSLE comes flying through.

BOOM!

The explosion sends them flying back, rendering them all UNCONSCIOUS.

When the smoke clears, an injured Piers looks up in terror.

THE SHADOW WALKS DOWN THROUGH THE HOLE FROM ITS SHIP, BRANDISHING THE STORM-REAPER.

[Reference Song: 'White Rabbit' by Jefferson Airplane plays.]

PIERS
No...

SHADOW
Piers King. Darkness has arrived.

ALANA
NO!!!!

Alana charges Shadow, but the Storm-Reaper lunges at her. It wraps its coils around her neck and slams her down to the ground, CHOKING her.

Shadow walks towards a defenseless Piers, picks him up, and throws him through the wall. He slides across the floor. Shadow marches toward Piers.

The Storm-Reaper DRAGS Alana through the hole in the wall.

SHADOW
They call you a hero. They call you their creator. But I know who you truly are. I know the sad, weak, defenseless boy.

PIERS
Please...stop. I'm begging you!

The weapon TIGHTENS its grip around Alana. She's dying.

ALANA
(weakly)
Piers...help...

SHADOW
You're weak! You're nothing but a burden!! Stand and fight me, boy!! Stand and fight, so you can see how pointless your struggle is. Fight me and I'll strike you down like your father and his before him!!

Piers screams as he charges Shadow with his sword. The Storm-Reaper unleashes from around Alana's throat and moves to Shadow's hands. The two CLASH their weapons.

Their fight rages on, Shadow barely having to try. It toys with Piers, adding to his sense of hopelessness.

SHADOW (CONT'D)
You are nothing!! You're a fraud!!

Shadow strikes him, breaking his sword and sending him flying back.

PIERS
Please... I give up. Please just stop.

SHADOW
Have you even considered the thought that maybe you're not even a good writer?!
(MORE)

SHADOW (CONT'D)
An ancient society of warrior women? A cyberpunk rock star? A stoic cowboy?! You have nothing new to offer anyone! You think people will read your stories? There's nothing original about them!

PIERS
Please! Stop! I can't take it anymore! Make it stop!!

Piers cries in pain. Shadow takes his Ion Board and SNAPS IT IN HALF. It strikes him back again.

SHADOW
You're not a writer! You're not special! You're a hack! You copy! You steal! You're not smart! You're not clever! And you're not a hero! You really think for a second that these...these cardboard cutout characters with false depth would follow someone like you?! They haven't even told you the truth about who they really are! They've lied to you this entire time!

PIERS
What?

SHADOW
(scoffing)
Of course, you don't know. You think you've brought color back to this world? You think you've saved it? As long as I still breathe, all the color you bring into this world...all the people you think you save will all be an illusion, just like your delusional, misguided, pretentious self. Killing you will be doing the world a favor!

Piers gets on his knees. He looks up and sees the other heroes stumble in the distance.

He closes his eyes and accepts his fate. But then-

CERRA HITS SHADOW OVER.

CERRA
Run! Get out of here!

Piers gets up and runs toward the heroes.

RICKY
CERRA! NO!!!

The Storm-Reaper shoots out toward Piers, but Cerra grabs it by its end, holding it back.

CERRA
GO!!!

As the ship collapses even further, the heroes drag Ricky back as he screams and yells.

Piers is carried out. Cerra fights a losing duel in the distance.

INT. THE ODESSA - BACK HANGAR - DAY

The heroes stumble into the hangar and board another dropship as fires spread throughout the ship.

EXT. THE ODESSA - DAY

The ship flies off into the sky. They look out as the Odessa explodes and crashes in the distance.

EXT. THE CLIFFS - DAY

The heroes sit on a rocky desert cliffside overlooking The Stone Plains. Giants in full color roam in front of them. Piers, his body bloody, bruised, and wrapped in bandages, stands over the edge.

RICKY
I can't believe she's gone. What am I going to do?

PIERS
I don't know, Ricky? What are you going to do? Yell at me? Hurt me? I'd like to see you try!

Piers turns toward the group.

PIERS (CONT'D)
I'll tell you all what you're going to do. You're going to tell me the truth! I want to know what Shadow was talking about!! What are you keeping from me?!

ALANA
Piers, please...

PIERS
No, Alana! I'm done! I've done too much for you all to be lied to again!

Silence.

PIERS (CONT'D)
TELL ME!!

They all look at him.

ALANA
Is he ready?

MONTANA
We don't got a choice.

PIERS
What? Ready for what?

ALANA
Piers...where do you think you are?

PIERS
I don't know...some world where all the characters and places I wrote about exist together?

ALANA
Who do you think we are?

PIERS
(confused)
I told you...you're characters I wrote.

ALANA
We're not where you think we are.

Piers looks around, confused, and scared.

ALANA (CONT'D)
This isn't a world where characters from your scripts and stories have come to life.

PIERS
I don't understand. What are you trying to tell me?!

ALANA
Just think, Piers. Really think
about what's happening.

The realization hits him.

PIERS
Oh my God. None of this is real.
It's all in my head.

RICKY
I knew we shouldn't have told him.

ALANA
Shut up, Ricky.

He looks at all of them. He can't believe what he's hearing. It's too much.

PIERS
Why didn't you tell me? I've been
with you guys for an entire month
and you never told me!!

ALANA
We thought if you became lucid of
the situation too early, your mind
would collapse in on itself. Then
all of this would be for nothing.

PIERS
What is this for, anyway?! What are
you doing to me? I thought I was
brought here to save all of you!

ALANA
No, Piers.
(beat)
We're trying to save you!!

PIERS
Get away from me!! Let me go!!

Piers pushes past them and runs down the cliff.

RICKY
So...we just gonna let him run?

MONTANA
Give the boy time, Ricky.

RICKY
Well, we're running out, Montana. The catalyst will happen in a matter of days, and then there won't be any Piers left TO save! We need a plan!! I knew we shouldn't have told him!!

ALANA
We'll find a way. We always do.

EXT. THE STONE PLAINS - DAY/NIGHT

Piers anxiously wanders The Stone Plains. He walks alone for DAYS.

Everything around him looks as if it's fading away. Panic settles in as reality fades away from him.

Piers falls to the ground.

The darkness surrounds him once again. Shadow appears, watching him. Piers' eyes go dark as if he's in a trance.

PIERS
I am nothing. I am nobody. I am worthless. I am the darkness.

But when it seems like all is lost, a sliver of light passes through the darkness. Alana, bathed in light, walks up to Piers. She holds him close.

ALANA
Remember who you are, Piers. You are not the darkness. You're a fighter, a writer, a rock star, and so much more. The darkness within you will NEVER define who you are. There's a light inside of you. Let it out.

Piers looks up and the darkness slowly fades. Soon, everything returns to normal. He looks up at her, shaking with fear.

PIERS
Alana, I can't do this. It's too much. I can't do this alone.

ALANA
That's the thing, Piers. You're not alone. You never were.

Alana helps Piers up.

And that's when he sees it.

SCORES of Stone Giants kneel before him. They carry all of the side characters from every location in their hands, letting them down onto the ground in front of Piers.

Celeste and the armies of Mrak stand in front of him. Varnish, Horace, and the rebels of Neo-Tokyo stand in front of him. Bonnie, Finlay, Domino, and the Wolf-Pack stand in front of him.

PIERS
(tears in his eyes)
No shot.

Alana and Celeste step forward, bearing GIFTS from Mrak.

CELESTE
As a showing of our gratitude for your efforts, I want to gift you the finest Mrakian armor from our palace, fitted just for you.

Montana, Bonnie, and Finlay step forward. Montana gives Piers his PONCHO and SIX-SHOOTER.

MONTANA
You earned them, Hoss.

Bonnie and Finlay give him a NECKLACE with a small horn on it.

FINLAY
Blow on it!

Piers blows, and his own GIANT WOLF comes out from the Wolf-Pack crowd and stands by him.

FINLAY (CONT'D)
(winking)
His name's Sherman!

BONNIE
Welcome to the Wolf-Pack, Piers.

They all look toward Ricky, Varnish, and Horace. Ricky shrugs.

RICKY
What? I already gave you the drumsticks!

Piers grabs the drum sticks from his jeans.

They MAGICALLY CHARGE UP and fly around his head, much like Shadow's Storm-Reaper. He grabs them, sticks them together to make a small staff, and then clips them back to his pants.

VARNISH
Hey, Piers. Check this out.

Varnish throws him a sleek new ION BOARD.

VARNISH (CONT'D)
Figured you could use an upgrade.

The Mrakian armor morphs to his body. He flips the six-shooter around his finger before holstering it. He throws the poncho around his back and it flows in the wind like a superhero's cape. The Ion Board snaps to his back.

RICKY
So what's the next move, boss? The Catalyst happens tomorrow.

Piers looks back on his army.

PIERS
It's time to finish the fight.

INT. SHADOW'S CASTLE - MAIN BUILDING - THRONE ROOM - NIGHT

Shadow meditates in its throne room. A black energy force surrounds it, engulfing the entire room in a deep darkness.

EXT. THE STONE PLAINS - NIGHT

Piers and his army march across The Stone Plains. Stars and binary moons light the night sky. All is silent but the marching of boots and the wind.

SHADOW (V.O.)
The time has come to face your destiny, Piers.

PIERS
(to himself)
I'm ready.

EXT. SHADOW'S CASTLE - THE DRIED DESERT - DAY

Piers and his army gather on The Dried Desert outside of Shadow's Castle. Ricky, Montana, Alana, and Abigail are all in front, serving as his lieutenants.

Everything is in COLOR besides the castle itself, which is still BLACK AND WHITE.

DARK ENERGY radiates from the castle's walls, polluting the air. Blots of BLACK DUST fall on the battlefield. The ground cracks and breaks beneath the castle's weight.

In the distance, Shadow's army of Cyber-Samurai gathers around the castle.

RICKY
Piers?

PIERS
Yeah?

RICKY
Don't tell anyone this...but I'm really scared.

PIERS
I know you are. Cause I am too.

He gets close to Ricky.

PIERS (CONT'D)
But now isn't the time for fear. It's time to be strong.

RICKY
For Cerra.

PIERS
For Cerra.

Piers rides in front of his army.

PIERS (CONT'D)
I wish I could say I'm one for speeches, but I'm sure you all know more than anyone that I've never been much of a talker. I'll try and keep this short...uh...

He turns and looks back toward the Cyber-Samurai armies, eyes wide with fear.

PIERS (CONT'D)
(to himself)
Be strong.
(to armies)
For too long, The Shadow has reigned over us. For too long, it took the color from our world. For too long, it turned our lives to dust. The foods we used to love tasted like nothing. The friends we spent our days with became enemies. The world moved around us, but we stayed still. It destroyed our motivation. It made us want to sleep without waking. It took all meaning from our lives and replaced it with crushing apathy.

His army stomps and slams their weapons down with passion.

PIERS (CONT'D)
For too long, we believed we were nothing but burdens. For too long, we lost faith in ourselves. For too long...we were worthless. All my life I stood by and let it break me down because I believed fighting it was pointless. But saving myself from this is the most important thing I will ever do. The Shadow took my father from me. It took my grandfather. But it will NOT take me. It will NOT take us. IT WILL NOT TAKE US!!

Piers turns to face the Castle.

THE ARMY
IT WILL NOT TAKE US!! IT WILL NOT TAKE US!!

PIERS
IT WILL NOT TAKE US!!!!

[Reference Song: 'Tom Sawyer' by Rush plays.]

With a final HOWL, Piers heroically leads his army into battle. He madly fires off his six-shooter, his poncho blowing in the wind.

The Wolf-Pack howl like crazy as they engage in battle once again.

The Mrakians charge valiantly into the fray, using their superior height and strength to even the odds.

The Stone Giants smash any air support that the Cyber-Samurai throw at them.

The original party of heroes fights with all they got, slowly making their way toward the castle. Each hero gets to have their own badass moments.

INT. SHADOW'S CASTLE - THRONE ROOM - DAY

The doors to the throne room swing open. A trio of Cyber-Samurai awaits orders.

SHADOW
Let the heroes come. They will face me alone.

EXT. SHADOW'S CASTLE - DRIED DESERT - DAY

The heroes fight outside massive castle walls.

PIERS
We need to get past the walls!

ALANA
Try asking one of the big guys!

Piers looks up at one of The Stone Giants. He activates his Ion Board and FLIES through the air, barely dodging laser fire from Cyber-Samurai attack ships.

A blast knocks him off the board, but he grabs onto it with one hand. He holds on until he falls onto the shoulder of a Stone Giant.

He gets up, reactivates his board, then flies in front of The Stone Giant.

PIERS
HEY! LOOK AT ME!

He points toward the wall.

PIERS (CONT'D)
SMASH!

The Stone Giant makes a deep groaning sound in agreement. It pushes forward to the massive wall, SMASHING A HUGE HOLE in it. The army lets out a triumphant roar when this happens.

EXT. SHADOW'S CASTLE - PALACE - DAY

Piers flies back down, joining the army. they begin to crowd into the palace. The main four heroes, along with all the supporting heroes, make it inside.

PIERS
Come on!!! We're almost there!!

As more warriors get through, three Stone Giants rip through the walls.

But then, A DARK BEAM OF ENERGY shoots into the sky.

ALANA
What the-

PIERS
That can't be good.

Out of the beam, a MASSIVE DARK ENERGY SHIELD forms around the castle.

RICKY
Oh no...

PIERS
EVERYONE! GET INSIDE! HURRY!

As the shield comes down on the Stone Giants, it SLICES them cleanly into pieces. Their bodies collapse onto the palace.

The heroes look up in fear.

PIERS (CONT'D)
TAKE COVER!

They all begin to take cover as pieces of the three Stone Giants fall. The heroes are helpless against the falling debris as it DECIMATES the buildings of the palace.

EXT. SHADOW'S CASTLE - PALACE RUINS - DAY

Darkness. Muffled screams. Then, cracks of light. Abigail stands over Piers. He's covered by debris.

ABIGAIL
I found him!!

Montana rushes over and helps him up, hugging him.

MONTANA
Are you hurt?

PIERS
Is it that obvious?

Finlay drags an injured Bonnie out of the rubble. Ricky and Varnish help an injured Horace get to safety. Alana searches for Celeste.

ALANA
Mother?! Mother?!

Nothing...until...she finds pieces of Mrakian armor on the ground. She quickly clears the debris in the area, panicking. Then, she finds Celeste. The queen lies in rubble, gravely injured.

CELESTE
(weak)
Alana.

ALANA
(on the verge of tears)
Mother! It's going to be alright. You'll be okay.

She grabs Alana, pulling her close.

CELESTE
No, my daughter. My destiny lies here. Yours lies with the Castle...and with Mrak.

ALANA
(crying)
No, Mother. I can't do it. Not without you. I'm not ready.

CELESTE
Yes, you are. You always have been. I'm proud to call you my daughter.

Celeste closes her eyes, passing away. Alana sobs.

PIERS
Alana!

Piers runs to her. He holds her as she cries.

A moment of silence follows as the heroes pay their respects to the legendary Mrakian Queen. But then-

Blood-curdling screeches ring through the palace.

Something is coming.

RICKY
Guys...we need to think of something quick.

PIERS
(taking charge)
Abigail, I want you down here protecting the wounded. Try and find a way to break through those shields. Alana, Ricky, and Montana...you're with me. We're going after the Shadow...together.

ABIGAIL
Good luck, Piers. We believe in you.

PIERS
Thank you.

MONTANA
(to Abigail)
Be careful.

ABIGAIL
(winking)
Always.

They nod, and the heroes run through the destroyed palace on their way to the main building.

Abigail gathers the injured heroes...Bonnie, Finlay, Varnish, and Horace...by the walls of the energy shield. Roars are heard in the distance.

ABIGAIL (CONT'D)
I hope they hurry.

HORACE
Give em' as much time as they need. I'm not afraid of a good fight.

FINLAY
You said it, big guy.

VARNISH
I'm willing to die. Are all of you?

BONNIE
Aye, aye, sir.

They all nod, helping each other stand up.

Varnish takes a long drag from an e-cigarette.

VARNISH
Then let's give em' a fight they won't forget.

Out of nowhere, hordes of BLACK SHADOW CREATURES emerge from the ruins and charge the heroes like crazy. The heroes roar war cries as they leap into battle with everything they have left.

INT. SHADOW'S CASTLE - MAIN BUILDING - HALLS - DAY

The heroes make their way through the castle until they reach the doors to the Throne Room. They all stop for a moment before going in, taking deep breaths.

PIERS
This is it.

Piers looks back at the three manifestations of himself standing before him.

PIERS (CONT'D)
There's a very real chance we won't make it out of this alive. Any last words before we go in?

ALANA
The Shadow has taken someone or something from all of us. Let's make it pay.

MONTANA
Like I've said before, even if we lose, there's something criminals and bad guys never understand. Truth and Justice always prevail.

They all look at Ricky.

RICKY
(reflective)
It's been one hell of a ride. I think we all owe you a thank you, Piers. Without you, shrimp, we'd all still be lost.

PIERS
I owe you guys, too. You all make me who I am.

ALANA
Along with so much more.

They all look at each other...one last time.

PIERS
Let's finish this. Together.

INT. SHADOW'S CASTLE - MAIN BUILDING - THRONE ROOM - DAY

The heroes smash through the door of the Throne Room. Shadow stands from its meditative state.

SHADOW
All of your failure, every mistake, every regret, every wrong decision you made in your life has brought you here. All of you against all of me. Who you think you are against who you really are.

PIERS
Your reign ends here, Shadow. I'm taking my mind back.

SHADOW
You can try, just as so many have tried and failed before you. Because the more you try, the more you fear yourself, the stronger I become.

PIERS
That's what you don't understand. I'm not afraid anymore.

SHADOW
Then show me, and I'll give you a reason to fear again.

The heroes howl war cries as they clash with the Shadow. The battle is fierce, intense, and brutal.

EXT. SHADOW'S CASTLE - PALACE RUINS - DAY

The injured supporting heroes fight in a brutal battle for survival in the palace ruins. Surrounded, outnumbered, and exhausted, it won't be long until the Shadow Creatures overcome them.

ABIGAIL
Come on, Piers. We believe in you.

INT. SHADOW'S CASTLE - MAIN BUILDING - THRONE ROOM - DAY

Piers pushes against Shadow with all he has. He fights harder than he's ever fought before.

But it's not enough. Shadow BEATS DOWN all the heroes, leaving them broken and exhausted on the ground.

SHADOW
I AM ENDOGENOUS, PIERS. I AM WITHIN YOU! I WILL NEVER LEAVE YOU, AND YOU CAN NEVER BEAT ME! NEVER!

Ricky looks on from across the room as Shadow pummels Piers. The Storm-Reaper wraps around Piers' neck, SUFFOCATING him.

SHADOW (CONT'D)
FEAR ME!!

Piers desperately gasps for air.

RICKY
(to himself)
Live for more.

Ricky yells as he sprints toward Shadow and tackles it. The Storm-Reaper releases from Piers and makes its way towards Ricky.

Shadow grabs Ricky by the neck and pulls him close.

SHADOW
A truly valiant effort.

The Storm-Reaper PIERCES Ricky's chest, and his body drops to the ground.

SHADOW (CONT'D)
But it is done in vain.

The heroes scream and cry as Ricky lies motionless on the ground.

SHADOW (CONT'D)
Useless boy.

Piers looks up with fiery anger.

SHADOW (CONT'D)
Time to end this useless fighting, Piers.

INT. MINDSCAPE - DAY

Shadow and Piers teleport to a black mindscape. Black tendrils tie Piers down to his knees.

MOMENTS FROM PIERS' LIFE begin playing all around him. They show his world in Black and White.

SHADOW
Look around, boy. You've wasted your life. Destroyed it beyond repair. You're lost in your own confusion.

Piers observes his surroundings.

SHADOW (CONT'D)
I'm not here to kill you. I'm here to set you free. I am nature taking its course. Your mind has given in. It's time for your body to follow. It's the only thing keeping you in this...prison.

PIERS
No. I won't do it!

SHADOW
What difference does it make? You want to live a life where your only desire is its end?

The screens begin playing his father's funeral.

SHADOW (CONT'D)
Follow your father's example. It's time to let go. You've lost everything! Your will is broken! Give in! Be strong! Do what you know is right!

PIERS
(struggling)
No! I'm still here!

The tendrils let go of Piers, setting him free.

SHADOW
Then strike me down.

Shadow throws the Storm-Reaper down at Piers' feet. He picks it up and stands, but he can't make himself walk toward Shadow. He just can't do it.

He falls back down, dropping the blade.

SHADOW (CONT'D)
Do you see now? You lack the will to choose. So let me choose for you. You're alone, Piers. GIVE IN! End the charade! End this false hope! I know who you are underneath! GIVE IN!

Piers stares up at Shadow. The MOMENTS begin to CHANGE. They begin showing his roommates, his scripts, his stories, his music, his longboard, and Sherman.

They begin showing the other heroes. They show his journey...the highs, the lows, and everything in between.

Piers rises up and grabs the Storm-Reaper. He marches toward Shadow.

SHADOW (CONT'D)
What is this?

PIERS
I'm the master of my own mind, Shadow. This is my world.

SHADOW
NO!

Shadow calls Storm-Reaper, but it won't move. It belongs to Piers now.

PIERS
NO MATTER WHAT, I WON'T GIVE IN. I WON'T LET YOU TAKE ME! NOT NOW! NOT EVER!!

Shadow falls to its knees as it loses its power. The black mindscape progressively turns to white.

PIERS (CONT'D)
I won't let you control me anymore!

The mindscape collapses until they are back in the-

INT. SHADOW'S CASTLE - MAIN BUILDING - THRONE ROOM - DAY

Piers stabs Shadow with the Storm-Reaper.

But nothing happens. Shadow laughs.

PIERS
What?

SHADOW
I told you, boy. You can't rid every darkness within you by stabbing it to death. I can't be killed. There is no cure. I'm a part of you forever.

PIERS
That's not possible. That's not how it works. It can't be. I'm the hero. I have to win.

SHADOW
I am lifelong, Piers. I will be with you until the day you die. The only way you can get rid of me is by getting rid of yourself.

Piers drops the Storm-Reaper and steps back, confused.

SHADOW (CONT'D)
You've lost. You never had a chance. As long as I'm alive, your life will never have color.

For a moment, Piers feels as if all hope is lost. But then, he comes to a realization.

PIERS
You're wrong.

The Storm-Reaper slithers toward Shadow.

PIERS (CONT'D)
You may be a part of me forever, but that doesn't mean I can't be happy.

The weapon wraps itself around Shadow like a cobra, dragging it back toward the throne.

SHADOW
I'll be back! It could be next week or twenty years from now. You can't imprison me forever!

PIERS
I think I'll manage.

Shadow yells as the Storm-Reaper locks it to the throne, covering it in a giant cocoon until its screams are nothing but muffled noise.

Piers nearly collapses from the battle, but he has no time to rest. He immediately runs to Ricky and the others.

RICKY
Did we win?

PIERS
(tearing up)
Yeah, buddy. We did.

RICKY
Did I go out like a hero?

PIERS
Yeah, you saved my life.

RICKY
Good. The Mrakian chicks are gonna love that.

They all laugh and cry.

RICKY (CONT'D)
(chuckling)
You owe me one, shrimp.

They all laugh again. Ricky's body slumps over in Piers' arms.

He passes away, eyes closed.

As he dies, color is restored to his body, as well as every hero.

EXT. SHADOW'S CASTLE - THE DRIED DESERT - DAY

[Reference Song: 'Layla' by Derek and the Dominoes plays, starting with the piano solo.]

The heroes walk out into the Dried Desert where they are greeted by the supporting heroes and the rest of the army. Piers carries Ricky's body.

They all stand in the desert, silent after their somewhat pyrrhic victory.

Dark clouds crowd the sky. The exhausted army anxiously readies itself for one last battle against the darkness. But then-

RAIN falls. It covers the entire landscape, and nearly instantaneously, GRASS grows.

Everyone stands and stares in glorious wonder, many of them seeing rain for the first time.

INT. VARNISH'S BAR - NIGHT - DAYS LATER

All the heroes and members from each faction are gathered in the bar. They dance and celebrate their victory in honor of Ricky. There is a memorial dedicated to him.

Alana grabs a drink from the counter from Horace and brings it outside.

EXT. VARNISH'S BAR - FRONT PATIO - NIGHT

Alana walks out to Piers. He broods.

ALANA
Hello.

PIERS
Hey. How are you doing?

ALANA
I'm okay, all things considered.

PIERS
I'm sorry about Celeste.

ALANA
She died for something she believed in. It's the most honorable thing a Mrakian can do. And she trusted me. I just hope I can be as good as she was.

PIERS
You can be better. I know you can.

Montana and Abigail walk out.

ABIGAIL
We were wondering where you went.

PIERS
Just getting some fresh air, that's all.
(beat)
So what are you guys gonna do now?

MONTANA
Abigail and I are fixin' to return to Keda where we belong. Them kids gon' need all the help they can get.

PIERS
(chuckling)
Yeah. They will.

Piers looks like he's about to cry.

PIERS (CONT'D)
I'm sorry, I just...I don't understand. We won, didn't we? Why don't I feel any better than before?

Alana looks back toward Montana and Abigail.

ALANA
Give us a second.

They leave. She takes Piers' hand.

ALANA (CONT'D)
Close your eyes. I want to show you something.

Piers closes his eyes and-

EXT. MRAK - THE LOOKOUT - NIGHT

Piers and Alana appear in the clouds. The moonlight shines on them.

ALANA
I know it's hard, that sense of unfulfillment you feel.

PIERS
Do you?

ALANA
Of course. I'm you, remember?

PIERS
(chuckles)
Yeah, I forgot about that.

Alana takes a few moments to appreciate the landscape.

ALANA
It's beautiful, isn't it? And it's all yours.
(pointing to her head)
It's all in here.

PIERS
I don't get what you're trying to say.

ALANA
I'm trying to say that your mind is capable of some pretty amazing things, Piers. Your mind is special. It has something to offer the world.

PIERS
Then why do I feel this way? What's wrong with me?

ALANA
As much as we'd like to think so, life's problems don't have simple solutions. You can't just beat the bad guy, save the day, get the girl, and expect everything to be perfect. Love isn't a magic potion that fixes all things.

PIERS
So what? All of this was for nothing? All the struggle, all the things we endured...Ricky's death...just for nothing to change?

ALANA
You'll find that life often lends itself to complexity rather than to answers. It's hard, Piers, and I wish I could give you some kind of answer. All I can be is here for you. I know that it seems like the challenges you face are insurmountable.

Piers chuckles.

PIERS
At least I did get the girl.

Alana blushes and laughs, covering her smile with her hand.

ALANA
Piers, shut up!

PIERS
I'm sorry. I just...I thought this would fix everything. I don't know what to do anymore.

ALANA
Look... sure, one book you read, one movie you watch, one girl you meet...it's not gonna fix your entire life. But that's not a bad thing. Your soul is a work of art that's never finished. Self-Discovery is a never-ending process, and that's why it's so beautiful. You're never going to be fully colored...because you'll always be coloring. This was just the first step...realizing you're not alone with yourself.

PIERS
And what if that self-discovery leads me somewhere dark?

ALANA
Like you said, Piers. Sometimes it just rains.

Thunder strikes and rain pours onto them as they stand on the clouds.

ALANA (CONT'D)
Just make sure you have this.

She hands him an UMBRELLA.

He opens it up and covers both of them. They look into each other's eyes.

She pulls him close and they kiss.

Piers smiles as he backs away and looks out into the night sky.

PIERS
This is the part where I go back home, isn't it?

ALANA
Yes, it is.

PIERS
What if I don't wanna go back? What if I wanna stay here with you, Montana, and Abigail. In here, I'm a hero. What's out there for me?

ALANA
There's so much in store for you in your world, Piers. You just haven't seen it yet.

Alana and Piers lock eyes, then-

MONTANA (O.S.)
She's right, Piers.

Piers looks to the side and sees Montana, Abigail, Finlay, Bonnie, Varnish, and Horace all standing on the clouds.

MONTANA (CONT'D)
You brought color to this world, son. Now it's high time you brought color to the other.

Piers goes and hugs Montana.

PIERS
I'm gonna miss you, Montana.

MONTANA
Don't worry now, Piers. We'll see each other again soon enough.

Piers looks out at all the heroes and waves goodbye.

ALANA
Piers?

He turns and looks at Alana. They walk to the edge of the cloud.

ALANA (CONT'D)
When you're ready...jump.

PIERS
I'm ready.

Piers looks down.

ALANA
Hey, Piers.

He looks back.

ALANA (CONT'D)
I love you.

PIERS
I love you too.

He jumps off the cloud and falls through the sky.

Led by the Fairy, all the creatures of Keda fly around him in a glorious display as he falls. He closes his eyes and smiles as they sing and dance around him.

INT. **PIERS' APARTMENT - PIERS' BEDROOM - MORNING**

[Reference Song: 'Let It Be' by The Beatles plays.]

Piers wakes up at his desk. He takes a minute to get used to the real world.

Alex knocks on the door and lets himself in.

ALEX
Hey, Piers. How you feeling?

Piers runs to him and hugs him.

ALEX (CONT'D)
Woah! You okay, buddy?

PIERS
Yeah, I am.

He holds the hug for a while, much to Alex's confusion.

ALEX
Piers?

Piers breaks the hug and looks at his roommate.

PIERS
I'm ready to get help.

Alex smiles.

INT. THERAPIST'S OFFICE - DAY

Alex and Piers sit in the lobby, Piers a little anxious. A THERAPIST walks out.

THERAPIST
Hi! Are you Piers?

PIERS
Yeah, that's me.

THERAPIST
Nice to meet you! Come on back and we can get started.

Piers follows the therapist into his office. He sits in a comfy chair in the corner of the room.

THERAPIST (CONT'D)
So Piers, how are you feeling today?

Piers thinks deeply about what to say. His eyes wander, pondering over the events that have transpired the last month.

PIERS
I'm feeling ready.

Piers cracks a genuine smile, the first real one in a while.

CUT TO BLACK.

SUPER OVER BLACK SCREEN:

"YOU ARE HERE."

THE END.

www.ingramcontent.com/pod-product-compliance
Lightning Source LLC
LaVergne TN
LVHW050314160826
845677LV00014B/3395